Coming for You

DEBORAH ROGERS

ISBN 978-0-473-51345-0

TITLE: Coming for You

First worldwide publication 2020

Published by Lawson Publishing (NZ).

For Jenna. A true friend.

1

I hate this. This half life. This half foot. So I come here to forget. To the subway. To just sit and imagine all of the things. All of the netherworld places beneath my feet. The warrens and laneways and sewers and tunnels and secret entrances and exits. The underground people pulling their underground carts into even more underground places. The rats and snakes and blind feral cats lurking and leaping and scuttling. Along and beneath the hot iron tracks, way down below through the cracks in the walls and the holes in the ground.

I come to ride the trains. Late at night when there are not too many people around. When I can get a fix on who exactly is in the car. When there's enough empty space to escape if I have to.

I get on anywhere and just sit and let the train take me away. I like the slipping and sliding on the blue plastic seat, the push and shove of the stop and start, the jerking and rolling, the thump of the wheels on the track. I like how no one looks at me and I don't have to look at them. I like how I can forget who I am and who I was meant to be and the gaping canyon between the two. I like how I don't have to think about the present, future, or past. Especially the past.

I ride and ride and ride. Sometimes for hours. I ride until the stale air tightens my face and the strange heartbeat of the train quiets my mind. I ride until all the thinking and dark thoughts abate. That's the goal anyway. Because if I'm honest, he never really goes away. My constant unwanted companion, who tumbles around my skull like a lone sneaker in a dryer, the rubber fixing to blister and melt in the heat of the barrel. He never lets go of me and I never let go of him. We are Siamese twins. Bound together by the crimes he committed against me and my soul.

But at least here on the train I can sit and pretend he does not exist. And pretending is better than nothing. Pretending is all I've got and I want to hold on to that for as long as I can.

I know the night's journey will end at some point and that I can't ride the train forever. After a few hours I will have to return to the real world above, where he does exist, and eventually I will, raising myself up from the seat to stand on my one good foot and steady my cane in my hand and clap myself out of the subway car and up the stairs and back into the savage world.

But for now, I am here, thinking and not thinking. For now, I can let myself breathe.

Tonight I count the number of people in the car with me. Three. A gray-haired woman in a fluoro jumpsuit and Birkenstocks sits opposite. A regular guy in blue jeans and a bomber jacket leans against the pole thumbing through his phone. A girl too young to be out this late on her own stands by the door staring into the flying darkness. I can see her face in the reflection and she catches me looking. She casts a sudden bold look at me over her shoulder as if to say what the hell are you looking at? I wonder what she sees in return, this woman with a cane in her sensible navy trouser suit. There goes one hell of a broken human being? A survivor? Am I survivor? Or did I really die back there in the woods?

I glance away and she returns to the window and the dark tunnel walls flip by.

Above me, someone has scratched the words *Pound Town* into the ceiling of the subway car. I imagine a youth in a hoodie teetering on top of the seat, arm hooked through the railing, stretching with a knife to carve those words into the steel. Maybe his friends goaded him on. Or maybe he was a loner like me and simply wanted the world to know he existed. I wonder if he ever returns to admire his work. If he stands amongst the rush hour commuters, quietly triumphant, holding his secret close.

The train pulls into a stop. I glance up, as I always do, checking for who's about to get on, and see them. A sea of expectant faces waiting on the platform. There are so many of them, so many faces, that I cannot possibly catalog each one. My heart pulses in my throat. The doors open and in comes the rush. All those chattering faces push their way in and fill up the car, swallowing up all that nice empty space. A well-to-do crowd in suits and tuxes and sequined dresses. In they come, pushing and laughing, fanning themselves with programs, diamante chandelier earrings swaying and winking. In they come, squeezing in on the seat beside me, standing around and over me, pressing in on all sides.

My throat goes tight. It's not safe. I'm no longer safe. Three has become dozens, all crammed together. They are too close. Everyone is too close. He is here. He is everywhere. I have to get out.

I wake up on the cold hard floor. In front of me, shoes, lots and lots of shoes, all pointing in my direction. Polished black oxfords. Brown leather loafers. Strappy Jimmy

Choos. High heels and kitten heels. A pair of battered Birks and an overgrown toenail.

I am flipped on my back. People loom over me.

"You dropped like a stone." A bald, rotund man in a blue sweater crouches next to me then tries to steady himself as the train rounds a corner. "I've never seen anything like it. I thought you were dead."

I turn my head. My cane's a few feet away. The Birkenstocks woman is eyeing it up. Take it, I want to say, go on, just take it, but I can't seem to speak, and now the man is lifting me to my feet and telling everyone to make room and the train stops and there's a swoosh of the doors and he ushers me across the threshold and onto the platform and we stand looking, me leaning on him, at the train waiting to depart.

"Don't miss it," I say.

"Oh, there'll be another one shortly."

But he wants to get on, I can tell. The doors close and he loses his chance. Instead he guides me to a row of seats, lowering me into the second to last one.

He hands me my cane. "Is there someone I should call?"

From the corner of my eye I see a flash of gold, his wedding ring, thinned by time, tightly wedged into the crease of his chubby digit.

I shake my head. "Not really."

He sits down. "What happened back there?"

"I'm not sure."

Another train pulls up and he tries not to look.

"Go on," I say. "I'm okay now. Thank you so much for your help."

"Someone should stay, make sure you're okay."

"Please, I'm fine."

He hesitates and casts a look of longing at the train.

"Go on, sir. Please."

He gets to his feet. "Well, if you're sure. My wife is waiting for me at home. Take care."

He hurries across the platform and ducks through the doors and stands looking at me through the glass as the train pulls away.

2

"You dropped like a stone."

I think of those words as I emerge from the subway. I'm shocked that it has happened again. I do the math in my head. Five weeks since the last episode. Three months before that. Seven months before that. They are becoming more frequent. I should be getting better by now but I'm only getting worse.

I pause to catch my breath at the top of the subway stairs. Stairs are the worst. Especially steep ones like these. I have to take them one at a time, steady my weight on the cane, haul myself up to the next one, all the while ignoring the pain shooting through my useless semi-foot. That's what they actually call it. A semi-foot. I nearly laughed out loud when I first heard the physical therapist say it during our sessions with the railings.

"That's right, Amelia, lead with your semi-foot."

They like to do that, the helpers, re-label disabilities and items to make them seem like less of a lack. Like my cane. They call it a device. An "assisted living device," to be more precise. Like the word "cane" is somehow derogatory.

Whatever its name, I'm still not used to my cane and the balance it requires. Three years since we were first introduced and I still make rookie mistakes. Like not taking enough care to ensure the rubber stopper at the bottom doesn't slip into a crack. Only last week, I careened face-first into the pavement right outside the courthouse.

Still, there are benefits. No one seems to bother a woman with a cane. If anything, people give me a wide berth because of it, as if I'm blind and they're worried I might walk straight into them. Once someone even tried to give me money.

I carry on to my apartment. I never take the same route home twice in a week. That could mean getting off a different subway stop and then taking a bus, or walking a few blocks (despite the pain), or getting back on the subway, or taking a cab. It's exhausting, constantly being on guard, thinking of the logistics for every journey home. But it's safer that way.

Outside it's as dark as ink and must be close to 1 a.m. And cold. Soon it will be fall. I don't like fall. There are too many reminders in the fall. In the fall I lose my hair. Strands litter the shower floor, stick to the bathroom walls, my pillow, the collar of my black woolen coat. It comes away in my fingers and fills the teeth of my comb. Not clumps exactly, but enough to worry that I might be afflicted with some strange form of seasonal alopecia. Enough to be concerned that the bald patches might never grow back. But they always do. In spring the molting stops and my hair renews. Grayer and more wiry than before. But at least it grows back.

"You dropped like a stone."

I think of myself lying there on the floor of the subway car, people staring at me, the Birkenstocks woman coveting my cane, the husband man helping me. At least there is still one kind soul in the world.

I reach the corner of 13th Street and 3rd Avenue and pause there. I can't decide which route to take. Every route seems risky tonight. The episode on the train has really

7

shaken me. Get a grip, I tell myself, so I choose left and skirt the empty basketball court and cross the road, then double back on the opposite side of the street and head east down 11th and into the alleyway. The alleyway is a narrow access path squeezed between two remodeled tenement buildings. It gives me the creeps but it's well-lit and will bring me out onto the avenue and into the postage stamp playground where I can take cover near the hedgerow to study my apartment building from afar.

I reach the playground and pause at the hedge to look at the building. It's a small eight-story walk-up, red-bricked with iron balconies and fire escape ladders, a former pencil factory converted into apartments back in the 1980s.

I scan the exterior and count four floors up. The new tenant in the floor below has put flowerpots and yucca plants on their balcony. I swear under my breath. Anyone could be hiding there and I wouldn't know it. And from there, they would only need to unclip the fire ladder and climb to my balcony directly above. But there's nothing I can do. People can't stop making their homes look nice just because of me.

There's a sudden movement to the left on the ledge outside the second-story apartment. I tense. Then I see the flick of a tail. It's only the cat, the no-name cat that nobody seems to own. I've seen it before, leaping from one balcony to the next or launching itself from the fire exit ladders to the floors below or above, like some kind of crazy ninja feline. One day that thing's going to slip and tumble headfirst right onto the pavement and its acrobat days will be over.

My eyes shift to my own apartment. The living room lights are on. I look at my watch. Just before two. The lights (two twenty-dollar floor lamps I bought on sale from Home Depot) are set on an automatic timer, and go on and off in pre-scheduled two-hour increments. A ruse so anyone outside would think there was someone home.

The windows are closed and both sets of venetian blinds are the way I left them this morning, hanging down at a precise midway point in the windowpanes, the slats open on a half-inch incline so the internal lights in the apartment shine through to the outside.

I wait there for at least twenty minutes, watching for movement inside the apartment. There's nothing. No one is in there. I am safe.

I emerge from behind the hedgerow and cross the road and head for the building, all the while fighting the urge to return to my hiding place in the playground to check on the apartment again.

It's not the first apartment I have lived in since the incident. There were four more prior to this one. On average I have shifted every six months. To stay ahead. To stay safe. When I have exhausted all the possible combinations of routes I can use to get to an apartment, I know I'm at risk of developing patterns and routines that could be detectable, so the only solution is to move again. Constantly shifting is exhausting and totally at odds with my nature to want to stay in one place. But I do it because there is no real alternative. I'd rather be a moving target than a sitting duck.

I reach the door to my building. It's a push code button type of lock where you key in a combination, but I'm smart enough to know that although this door is meant to be the first line of defense, it's really no defense at all. People can easily slip in behind someone else. Tenants can (and do) give out the code to friends and relatives. So I never trust it. The only real first line of defense is my own apartment door.

Before I key in the code, I glance over my shoulder to study the street. Empty. I slip inside and push the door firmly behind me until I hear the nib click back into place.

The stairwell is to my left. Empty and well-lit. Four flights of stairs are beyond my current capabilities, so I take the elevator instead. An old-fashioned Otis elevator with a scissor gate that no one else bothers to use. It stammers upward to my floor and I walk the six footsteps to my apartment door. I pause and listen as the elevator staggers back down to the ground floor. Someone is playing Xbox in one of the apartments above. A moan of a siren a few streets away.

I push my keys into the dead bolts in my door. There are two of them, state of the art, titanium models. I do not trust potentially corruptible tradesmen so I installed them myself, something I have become very good at from watching YouTube clips.

I unlock the door and stand on the threshold, listening. It's more than listening really. Sensing is a more accurate description, using my gut to get a read on the energy in the apartment, to detect whether someone is in there, invading my territory, filling it up. Tonight there is nothing. But this does not mean I can relax. No way. Now the real work begins.

I'm bone tired and desperate for sleep. I have a full schedule at work tomorrow and need to be on my game. But there's a detailed checking process I must follow before I can even think of going to bed. By now my Home Depot lights are off and I keep it that way. Leaving the front door open, I step inside. Back at the start of all this, after the incident and long stay at the hospital, when I first went to live on my own, when this process of checking began, I faced the dilemma of whether to leave the front door open while I checked the inside of the apartment. A dilemma because someone could sneak through the front door while I was deep in the apartment and carry out a blitz attack on me. But if I locked the door behind me before I checked the rest of the apartment and there *was* someone inside, it would mean I would be trapped in the apartment with them. That's when I came to realize that a good checking strategy was as much about escape as it was about entry. So when I moved here three months ago, the first thing I did was carefully map out the escape routes. Should the worst occur I have three available options:

1.   **Flee out my front door.** Activate the building's fire alarm on the landing. Bang on everybody's doors. Shout Fire! People come running. Attacker scared off. It's my number one strategy because with my foot how it is, I could never outrun the potential attacker. I could take the elevator, but by the time I got to the ground floor, he would be waiting for me at the bottom of the stairs and I'd be as good as dead.

2.   **Climb out the living room window.** Get onto the balcony. Unhook the fire escape and make my way down to the next level's balcony and fire escape and so on until I reach the ground. Not easy with my foot but I can do it. One time my neighbor caught me practicing. Mr. Lee from apartment 5b. He's been kind enough to look the other way ever since.

3.   **The last resort.** Not so much an escape strategy as a final solution. Shoot the fucker in the head with my

11

Glock 19 9mm compact semi-automatic pistol that I keep in the side table next to the sofa.

That's it. Only two escape routes out of the apartment, and one last resort, but at least I have a plan.

I cross the living room floor and check that the large window overlooking the balcony is firmly locked, that the venetian blinds have not been touched, that no dust has been stirred. After that, I hang back behind the window frame, look out the window and onto the balcony, and study the dark street below. All clear. I lower the venetian blinds and adjust the slats until they are closed all the way, then walk the circumference of the room, checking that nothing's out of place, that the armchair and sofa have not been sat on or moved.

I head to my bedroom and check the window there. The latch holds firm, the way I left it this morning. The blinds are the same, too. I look around and check that nothing has been moved and it all looks okay. I pause and study my bedroom closet, or what's left of my bedroom closet. I removed the doors when I first came here. The thought of someone hiding inside made me on edge all the time, so I took them off.

It's tidy, with just the bare essentials to aid a clearer view. Everything from my old life is gone. All those frivolous dresses, too short and pretty for me now given my cumbersome foot. Not a high heel in sight, either. Now it's all about sensible orthopedic-adjusted shoes. Serious career pant suits and blazers. Besides, it's easier to get away in flats and trousers than a skirt and kitten heels.

I scan the racks. Two pant suits, one gray, one navy, both with matching blazers. Two neatly pressed white shirts. A beige raincoat and gray knee-length woolen coat complete the collection. Resting on the shoe rack below are two pairs of flats, black and black, and two pairs of Nikes with a special orthopedic insert, my gym bag next to those.

In the three cubby holes to the left, two sweaters and one hoodie sit neat and snug. Below that, a pair of jeans and sweatpants. My workout gear occupies the final cubby.

My eyes scan slowly left to right. It's still dark in there, I think, inside the closet. Despite my attempts at minimalism, I should throw more things out. But not tonight. Tonight I don't have the energy. My eyes reach the winter woolen coat and halt. Oh god, was that movement? Did I hear a breath? Did the hem of my coat shift ever so slightly? My heart begins to race.

I fight the urge to run. Instead, I tell myself to just calm the hell down and take another look. And when I do, I see that I'm wrong. Nothing there except the imaginings of my touchy amygdala. I lower myself onto the bed and take six full breaths to calm my rising panic. No one is there. No one is there. No one is there.

I look at the clock on the bedside table. It's after two. I need to get some sleep or I will be a wreck in the morning. I wonder what my colleagues at the DA's office would think if they could see me now, shaking, out of control, imagining phantoms in the wardrobe.

Heart still pounding, I get up and leave the bedroom. There's nothing to worry about, I tell myself, just finish checking then go to bed. I pause at the door of the spare room next to mine and turn the handle. It does not budge. Still locked. Good.

Next I move to the bathroom, check behind the shower curtain. All clear, so I head back to the front door and turn the knob and check the locks again. Then do the circuit twice more, rechecking the living room, my bedroom, the other room, the bathroom, the front door as thoroughly as I did the first time. Even after I have done the checking three times there is always the urge to check once more.

But I tell myself that everything is fine. The apartment is safe. I am safe. I have done enough for the night. I realize I am shivering. The apartment is freezing. I turn on the heat, twisting the thermostat way up. The crummy thing rattles into life, blows out stale air, but warms the place quickly.

I can barely keep my eyes open and head for my bedroom. A sudden high-pitched beep stops me. My cell phone battery is dying. I turn back and dig inside my purse to put it on the charger. The screen is lit with four missed calls. I listen to them. The first is from my mother. Would Amelia please keep her eye out for the vacation brochure on Bali she'd sent her, and wouldn't it be great if Amelia could meet a nice man to take because she'd heard there were fantastic resorts where you could get couples massages for a very good price. The second message is from Claire Watson, the New Jersey mom of the eleven-year-old child witness I am supposed to be briefing tomorrow. "Amelia? I need to talk to you. Give me a call." Blunt and to the point, in true Claire Watson fashion. Her message was left at 7:38 p.m. It's now nearly 2:30 a.m. Too late to call. It will have to wait until tomorrow. I swallow down the guilt, not sure how I'm going to explain my tardiness. The third is from Lorna. My therapist. She's pissed I missed our appointment. Twice. I look down at the fourth missed call and go cold. Number unknown. No message. It's nothing, I tell myself. I stare at the screen for a long time. It doesn't mean anything, nothing at all. But it's too late, it sets me off and I begin the checking all over again.

3

I hurry up Center Street and head toward the Civic Center District of Manhattan, finger-combing my unbrushed hair as I go. I'm late for my witness briefing with Susie Watson. The checking this morning has put me behind. It took me longer than normal to get out of the apartment because that stupid unknown call was still playing on my mind. I chide myself. I should be getting better but I'm only getting worse. It cannot go on like this. At the best of times, morning checking is generally worse than nighttime checking because of the time pressure to get to work. I hate rushing because I'm afraid I might make a mistake and overlook some critical detail. As a result, I have often found myself outside the apartment and the blinds don't look quite right so I have to go back and start the process all over again.

Case in point, this morning when I studied the apartment from the outside, doubts crept in. Were the venetian slats at the correct angle? Did I check the auto light timer was working? Did I look behind the shower curtain in the bathroom? I was torn about whether to return to the apartment or be late. Finally, I swallowed down my anxiety and headed for work. I could not let poor Susie down. The little girl had been through enough already.

I reach Foley Square and the New York State Supreme Court Building, the court where serious matters are heard, serious criminal matters like the one involving Susie Watson. The building makes me feel small, with its giant

Roman granite columns and sweeping stone steps leading up to the grand colonnaded entrance. I am just a limping ant with a cane. And one day this limping ant will get found out. Because I have the credentials, sure, the law degree, the will to do good, but sometimes it's hard not to think there's been some kind of a mistake. That I don't really belong here, trying cases, putting the bad guys away. Some days I feel like I'm an imposter who's making it up as she goes along, and today is definitely one of those days.

I pause and look across the road at Thomas Paine Park. It's quiet over there this morning, with just a smattering of people. An old-timer feeding pigeons. A twenty-something in jeans and heels getting coffee from a cart. A clean-cut Wall Street broker in a crisp Armani shirt heading to work.

I turn back to face the courthouse, take a breath to steal myself, and, one at a time, make my way up the steps. Leading with my one good foot, I stick close to the railing running up the middle to the colonnade in case my balance deserts me.

I make it to the top just as a single bead of sweat tumbles from my hairline. I swipe it away and enter the building through the ornate timber doors. I flash my Assistant District Attorney ID to security even though they know me by sight (there's not too many young female lawyers with a cane), and pass my satchel through X-ray. Sometimes they have tried to wave me through without the X-ray, thinking they are doing me a favor, but that makes me nervous, because if they are doing that for me who else is getting special treatment?

Claire and Susie Watson are waiting for me outside Courtroom No.7. Claire, the mom, a salt-of-the-earth, thick-waisted waitress, with a head full of curly black hair, is wearing her usual outfit. An old-fashioned pair of acid-wash jeans with a Budweiser T-shirt, tucked in, and a pair of soft-soled dirty blue sneakers.

Claire worked two jobs so she could send Susie to an exclusive private school called Ashbury Preparatory and Grammar School in the Upper West Side. Every day for nearly three years, the two of them had made the two-and-a-half-hour round journey from New Jersey to Ashbury.

"I wanted Susie to have a better life than my bullshit crappy one," Claire had told me when we first met. "You know, give her a proper start, so she could meet the right people, go places. Well, now I know better, don't I?" Claire had said bitterly through a haze of tears.

Because Mr. Alistair Kennedy was definitely not the "right people" and was now the reason why her daughter was in therapy once a week, possibly for the rest of her life, and about to testify against him in a court of law.

Next to her mom, Susie is looking slightly bewildered. She's wearing a violet-colored top with a frill around the bottom over a denim skirt, and her dark curly hair, just like her mother's although longer, hangs in a loose ponytail at the nape her neck. Susie is small for her age, looks more like nine than eleven (which won't hurt the case if I'm honest), and if it's possible, she looks even smaller today, as if the gravity of what she's being asked to do has finally made landfall on Susie's fragile young shoulders.

Standing with them is a man I don't recognize. Funny, I don't remember Claire mentioning a boyfriend.

By the looks of the scowl on Claire's face, she's angry about something. And when she sees me approaching, she doesn't waste any time telling me what's on her mind.

"Amelia, I called you and you never got back to me. I've been going out of my mind here. You gotta do something! This guy"—she gestures to the man with distaste, her New Jersey drawl even more evident given her current state of enragement—"it's just so freaking stupid."

Like me, the man looks like he's been up half the night. He's in need of a shave and, given the thick dark hair skimming the collar of his shirt, he could do with a haircut, too. Late thirties or early forties, older than me, broad-shouldered but stooped as if he was apologetic for taking up too much space. Good-looking in a tired sort of way.

He extends his hand. "Detective Ethan North." We shake. Warm, not too firm. He withdraws a little quicker than feels normal.

I'm puzzled. "Where's Detective Barker?"

Claire raises her arms, exasperated. "My point exactly."

Detective North shoves his hands in his pockets. There's a whiff of stale coffee and deodorant hastily applied.

"He was needed on another matter. I've been assigned to Susie's case now."

"At this late stage?" I say.

He rubs the knuckle of his forefinger along his upper lip where there's the silvery scar of a harelip repaired some time ago.

"Yes."

"But Detective Barker has been on this matter since the beginning. He has all the case knowledge. A change this late in the game is…well, quite frankly, it could be damaging to a successful conviction."

"That's what I keep telling him," says Claire, planting her hands on her hips.

"Don't worry," he says, "I'm up to date on the case file."
The reason for the crumpled shirt and lack of morning
shave, I suspect.

All at once, I'm sorry. This poor schmuck has nothing
to do with his stupid departmental decisions. He's just
another cog in the wheel like me.

"This isn't good enough," says Claire, jabbing a finger at
him. "My daughter deserves better."

He flinches slightly, then resumes a neutral expression.
"There's nothing I can do."

"It'll be okay, Claire," I say, conscious that Susie is only
a few feet away on the bench. "We're at the tail end of this
thing now. How about we just get started?"

Claire looks like she wants to argue some more. Instead,
she gives up. "I don't like it one little bit, Amelia. I really
don't. But I'm sane enough to realize that like most things
that have happened to me in my pathetic life there is jack
shit I can do about it." She takes Susie's hand. "Come on,
baby. Let's get this over with."

Detective North reaches for the door handle to the
interview room.

Claire swings round to face him. "Not you." She looks
at me. "I don't want him in there, Amelia."

"But Claire, Detective North has to be present to protect
the continuity of the case."

She shakes her head. "You can't expect Susie to talk
about what happened in front of a man she doesn't even
know. No way. Not gonna happen."

"But Claire—" I protest.

Detective North holds up his hand.

"I'll wait here," he says.

"Well, if you're sure," I say.

20

"He's sure," says Claire Watson. "Now are we doing this or what?"

4

Thanks to a favor from the court clerk, Barbara Hobbs, the long-serving bespectacled sixty-something courthouse matriarch who happened to feel sorry for me because of my disability, I have been granted access to courtroom No.7. My hope is to help demystify some of the trial process for Susie. Another hearing starts at 10 a.m. and we need to be out in twenty minutes, I'm told firmly by Barbara Hobbs. No exception.

The room is not one of the particularly grand courtrooms in the building. On the smaller side, it has the same dark wood paneling and boxy high windows typical of the other Supreme Court rooms, but this one's more intimate, or claustrophobic if you happen to be an eleven-year-old girl required to give evidence against your teacher. Both the defense and prosecution tables are relatively close to the witness box and judge's bench, and even the most confident of witnesses can find that unnerving. The public gallery, with its allotment of five rows of hardwood seating, is separated from the rest of the court by a wooden balustrade, or "the bar." The jury box is to the left of the judge's bench, and a tiny press gallery to the right.

Empty now, the room doesn't seem too threatening, but it can and does feel crowded depending on how many people attend. And it's likely to be a full house for the trial tomorrow, *People vs. Kennedy*. A teacher accused of sexual assault against a minor tends to draw a crowd.

On the plus side, the trial is likely to be short. Three days at the most, including the judge's summing up and the opening and closing arguments. On the negative side, the reason it will be so short is because all the witnesses have dropped out. One-by-one, like a slow leaking faucet. That's because after the initial complaints were laid, parents began to realize the terrible effects the process was having on their children. Not to mention the public scandal side of things. It was too much of a burden for them to bear. So they departed like rats from a sinking ship. Not that I blame them. I probably would have done the same thing.

So it was all down to little Susie Watson and me. I look at Susie now, sitting in the dark green leather-buttoned judge's chair, watching *Dance Moms* on my tablet, and think how crazy it is that this entire case hangs on the word of this child. Yes, there was some medical evidence but that was in no way foolproof, and the defense will seek to exploit any ambiguity in the medical examiner's interpretation of what she found when she saw Susie, months after the events.

Right now, Susie seems oblivious to it all, to the ordeal she will have to go through tomorrow. But kids do that, don't they? Pretend not to care, pretend everything is okay, when underneath they are positively rigid with fear.

"Thanks for letting her play with that," says Claire, nodding to the tablet. "She wants an iPhone. But she's a good kid. She doesn't pester me. Knows we can't afford it. Give Ms. Kellaway's iPad back, baby, and say thank you."

I look at Claire and Susie, this tight team of two, and feel a flash of envy. How will I ever be able to bring a child of my own into my messed-up world?

Susie hands me the iPad. "Thank you, Ms. Kellaway."

"You're welcome, Susie."

She gives me an uncertain smile and twists the beaded bracelet on her right wrist while she waits for me to begin. On her tiny clipped fingernails, there are remnants of faint blue nail polish from a mother-daughter pamper session sometime back. What was it like to be eleven, I wonder. Eleven and in this position. A little kid just trying to hold on to whatever childhood she can salvage in the midst of all this darkness. Both mother and daughter look at me expectantly, and I know they are hoping I can somehow fix what happened. Suddenly I feel the weight of the world on my shoulders.

I take out the trial briefing from my satchel. "Are you ready to go over your questions now, Susie?"

"What happened to your foot?" she says, without looking up from the bracelet she's twirling round her wrist.

"*Susie*," scolds Claire.

"No, it's okay," I say. "I had an accident."

Susie frowns, inspects a lime green bead with great interest. "Does it hurt?"

"Sometimes." I turn and look at the empty courtroom. "Susie, we need to run through what you're going to say tomorrow." I point to the witness box. "You'll sit right up here, but don't worry because there will be a screen so you won't be able to see him."

"Was it a car accident?"

"No, not a car accident. The screen means he won't be able to see you either."

Susie finally looks at me. "What kind of accident?"

"Listen to Ms. Kellaway, baby, what she's saying is important," says Claire.

I crouch to face Susie. "I got a splinter in my foot and it got infected. Susie, tomorrow I'm going to ask you questions. Then Mr. Kennedy's lawyer will ask you questions, too."

"A splinter's not an accident."

Claire throws her head back and blinks at the ceiling. "Susie, for the love of God."

I pause. "Would you like to see it?"

The girl's eyes widen and she nods.

"You don't have to do that," says Claire.

"It's fine."

I pull out one of the hardbacked chairs and sit down and slip off my orthopedic shoe and sock. Both Claire and Susie fall silent as they stare at my ugly half lump.

"It's not so bad," I say finally.

"You must be brave," says Susie.

I put my shoe back on and face Susie. "Well, tomorrow it's your turn to be brave."

"Can Mom sit with me?"

"No. But Annie the social worker will be there, standing right behind you in case you need anything. All you have to do is tell the court exactly what you told me. Then your job will be done and you can go home."

"I don't want to."

"It's going to be fine, Susie. You just need to tell the truth," I say.

"Will Mr. Kennedy go to jail?"

I nod. "I hope so. Will you do it for me, Susie? So he can't hurt any more girls?"

She looks at me. "Will it be like last time?"

I frown. "Last time?"

"When I was little, when the lady called me a liar and said I was making it up but I wasn't."

My foot begins to throb.

I look at Claire. "What's Susie talking about?"

Claire stares at me without speaking.

"Claire?"

"I was gonna tell you. I swear I was, but there was never a right time."

I feel a weight in my chest. "Tell me what, Claire?"

She pivots and presses her forehead to the wall. "Christ, I'm such a freaking idiot."

"Claire."

"It's ancient history, Amelia."

Suddenly I'm drained. "Has Susie made a similar accusation before?"

Claire hits the wall with her palm. Curses some more. I rub my hand over my face and long to lock myself inside the safety of my apartment.

"I'm going to ask you the question again, Claire. This time I need an answer. Has Susie made a similar accusation before?"

A barely perceptible nod.

"When?"

"Preschool. She was four."

"Where?"

"Seattle. I lived out there with Susie's father."

"They said I made it up," says Susie. "But I didn't, did I, Momma? You helped me remember, didn't you? I was telling the truth. That man Lucas touched me."

Claire begins to cry. "No, baby."

Susie frowns. "He did. I remember."

"No, baby. It was a mistake. Nothing happened to you."

Susie touches her mother's shoulder. "Don't cry, Momma."

The last thing I want is Susie getting distressed so I make a suggestion. "Hey, Susie, how would you like to play on my iPad again while I talk with your mom?"

Susie glances at her mother, uncertain.

Claire nods. "It's okay, baby. Go ahead."

I unlock my tablet, hand it to Susie, and steer Claire toward the last row in the public gallery.

"Talk to me, Claire," I whisper, my frustration rising.

She wipes the tears with the heel of her hand. "I'm sorry."

"Just tell me what happened."

"She was in day care because I had to work two shitty jobs. Her dumb-ass father had taken off for the first time and left me to do everything. I started hearing rumors about one of the staff. This guy named Lucas. I didn't trust him so one night I questioned Susie. I know I wasn't supposed to, that only specialists should do that kind of thing, but I did it anyway. You gotta understand, I was just trying to protect my daughter. Then Susie started saying all this crazy stuff about how Lucas had touched her behind and made her kiss like people on the TV kissed. As I kept questioning her, the story just got worse and worse. I panicked and pulled her right out of the day care and went straight to the police."

"And they charged him? It went to court?"

There's a knock on the door. The court registrar pokes his head in. Behind him people are gathering.

"I need to set up," he says.

I glance at the clock. Ten before ten. "Five more minutes?"

He doesn't look happy.

"Please," I say. "We're nearly done here."

He rolls his eyes and mutters something under his breath but closes the door.

I turn back to Claire. "What happened with the case?"

She emits a long sigh. "It got thrown out. There were CCTV cameras in the day care that showed he couldn't have possibly done it." She looks down at her hands. "It was my fault, I see that now. I had my own abuse issues and I think it drove me to ask Susie more and more questions, leading questions. She was just giving me answers she thought I wanted to hear."

"Did you get money, Claire?"

Claire looks at me sharply. "What?"

"Compensation? A payout? Insurance of any kind?"

She's obviously sickened by the question. "What kind of mother do you think I am?"

I remain calm. "I have to ask. Were the accusations aimed at making money in any way?"

Claire looks like she might hit me.

"Of course not. No amount of money would make me put my own daughter through that."

Another knock. This time insistent. I get to my feet and open the door a crack.

"We'll be out in a minute," I say.

"I need to get started," whines the registrar. His front tooth on the right is going black at the root. I wonder if it hurts.

"I understand. Two minutes. Promise." I shut the door, ignoring the look of exasperation on his face.

"I never questioned her this time, Amelia. I swear. This time she came to me and told me everything. And it wasn't just Susie saying it, there were six other girls. You know that."

Yes. That was true. There was no doubt in my mind that Kennedy had done it. I had seen the evidence for myself. It was overwhelming. The catalog of the victims' injuries in the ME's reports. The consistency in the victims' statement. The child pornography found on his work computer.

I glance at Susie. Caught in the middle of all of this.

"You should have told me, Claire."

"I know. I'm sorry."

"This jeopardizes the whole case."

"It was so long ago and halfway across the country. I just wanted to put it behind us. Don't pull her out, Amelia. You know as well as I do Kennedy's as guilty as sin. He needs to be stopped and Susie deserves justice."

"This puts me in a very difficult position, Claire."

She grabs my hands between hers. "Please, Amelia. We've got to see this through. Please tell me I haven't royally fucked this up?"

The door bursts open. Barbara Hobbs appears in the void, hands on her substantial hips, face angry and red. She points a finger at me.

"You," she says. "Out. Now."

5

How they think I'm ever going to fix this. Me, the big lawyer. They don't even know. I spend most of the day in a haze trying to organize my thoughts. But it's a mess inside my head. The lack of sleep hasn't helped and the mind fog is worse than usual. And now this? A false allegation of sexual abuse from my one and only witness.

I've been sitting at my desk staring at the computer for two hours. My colleagues are too busy to notice. Knee-deep and lost in their own earnestness to change the world. That's why everyone works here in the New York District Attorney's Office, or mostly everyone, to help put the bad guys away, to do good. It's not about the money, that's for sure.

It's a busy, noisy open-plan office, but somehow I manage to shut it all out. Noise-cancelling headphones help. No one bothers me when I have them on and I focus better without all that sound. Usually. Because the headphones are not working today. Today I'm too much on edge.

I don't know what to do. The word DISCLOSURE flashes above my head like a neon sign. I should have reported Susie's admission by now, but I haven't. I have picked up the phone exactly three times to call the lead defense counsel Eileen Mercer but hung up before I was put through.

A year ago I wouldn't have questioned my duty to do this. I'm a sworn officer of the court and it's my obligation to uphold the law. Disclosure, full disclosure, is a fundamental part of the system, like the right to the presumption of innocence. It means there's a level playing field for everyone. The accused has a right to know all the details of the case against them. They certainly have the right to know a key witness has made false allegations in the past. It goes to credibility. And Mercer is a good lawyer. She would make a meal out of this.

Besides the duty thing, there are the practical implications. Should Kennedy get convicted, and if some way down the track the defense finds out about the lack of disclosure, the conviction would, in all likeliness, get overturned on appeal.

If they found out. And that was the thing. How would they ever know? Claire would never say anything. And the situation took place over seven years ago, far away on the West Coast. I think of Detective Ethan North. In the ruckus with the very cross Barbara Hobbs and incensed registrar with the bad tooth, I had managed to avoid him by rushing from the courthouse, muttering I needed to get to another appointment. I should really tell him. But the false allegation was seven years ago. Susie had been a toddler. It had been a mistake. And without Susie's testimony there will be no conviction for Kennedy. She is critical to the case. The testimony and evidence relating to the other girls could not be admitted because they had pulled out. Without Susie, not only will Alistair Kennedy get away with it, he will likely do it again.

And what would it do to Susie and Claire to not have their day in court? I remember when I first met them last year when I got assigned the case, how vulnerable they both looked. I could see through the veneer of Claire's "don't-give-a-shit" exterior in an instant. I recognized it for the self-preservation mechanism it was.

But it isn't my job to knowingly break the law. I'm just supposed to follow the rules and work within the system and I always have and I'm not sure why this time is any different.

So then, why don't I just pick up the goddamn phone?

I rub my temples and sit back in my office chair. I close my eyes and imagine riding the subway. The stale air and dirty breeze. The hollow sound of a half-empty car.

"Hey, Amelia. Your phone's ringing."

Jacob, at the desk next to mine, is shouting over the partition. I open my eyes and look at my vibrating phone. Mercer's number flashes up. I ignore it and it stops and I sit there thinking.

I look around the buzzing office, take in all the heartfelt, sincere intention imbued in the atmosphere like a cologne. I pick up my bag and go.

6

I turn left and clap my way up the street, fighting against a biting wind. The gym bag hooked over my shoulder is weighing me down, a counterweight upsetting the delicate balance I need to maintain upright and mobile. This is what I have had to relearn. How to walk in a different way than I did before. How to rely on a man-made instrument more than my own body. How not to think about the missing metatarsals and bone and cartridge. Or the toes that still itch even though they aren't even there.

I think back to the hot and cold water therapy. The painful exercises I had to do. The hatred I felt toward my cane. At the time I told myself that a disability would not define me. That I would be just like I was before, only without a full foot. That I would rise above what happened to me and move forward in my life a stronger, better, braver person.

But that was a lie. There is nothing brave about me at all.

Tonight was fifty/fifty between riding the subway or going to the gym. My first inclination was to ride the subway because I figured it might give me time to think through the disclosure dilemma. But I couldn't face the ugly possibility of passing out in some strange borough again (and not having the fortune of a portly gentlemanly savior like I had last night), so I elected to go to the gym instead.

As I do with my apartment, I mix up my routes to the gym. Because patterns and the usual are the Hansel and Gretel crumbs that could lead to my downfall.

Tonight I take two different trains and walk my way in and around the blocks surrounding the Port Authority Bus Terminal on the corner of 8th Avenue and 42nd Street. I head north toward Hell's Kitchen, dodging overstuffed trash bags piled in clumps on the curb, passing by the dingy steak houses and dimly lit bars and deep-fried aroma of greasy spoon joints. Wedged here and there, between the various restaurants, is the occasional eclectic boutique, selling vintage apparel like a pair of 1960s leather block-heeled pumps and tweed winter coat with a rabbit fur collar.

I keep walking until I reach a nondescript door halfway up a quiet alleyway and step inside. I pause there and take in the smell of well-used yoga mats and pine disinfectant. The fluorescent rod flickers overhead, illuminating the poster of Venus Williams in her purple Berlei bounce-less sports bra, stained by a water leak sometime back but never replaced. I hear a whoosh in the labyrinth of pipes lacing the ceiling as someone flushes the toilet.

I see Beth. Thank God for Beth. With her sober square face and frank eyes and broad shoulders. Thank God for the strength of her spine, so much stronger than mine, and the way her arm darts out whenever I'm about to fall, ready to catch me like a brace, then reposition me upright over and over. Thank God, too, for her unsmiling lips and her "I-don't-give-a-fuck-what-anyone-thinks-of-me-attitude," because that's why I trust her second only to myself.

We first met eighteen months ago when I spied the flyer on the noticeboard in the work cafeteria. Amongst the ads for secondhand cars, roommates wanted, private yoga sessions, and Reiki training was one for self-defense classes at a women's-only gym. It took me a month to decide whether or not to go. In the end, I did, which turned out to be one of my better ideas because I met Beth and Beth taught me many useful self-defense techniques I could master, even with a cumbersome half foot.

Tonight the gym is quiet because class does not start for another hour yet. I head for the changing rooms and spot Beth in the studio skipping like a maniac in front of the wall mirror. Her eyes shift to my reflection.

"Twice in one week," she says, not breaking a beat.

The black peony rose on her shoulder is slick with sweat.

"Yeah," I say. "Glutton for punishment."

"One-on-one?" she offers, thrusting her chin at the container of Everlast boxing gloves and mitts.

I nod. "Why not."

I go change and when I return, she's got the equipment out. The medicine balls, the gloves, but the rope is back on its hook because for me it's the sandbag across my shoulders and lunges back and forth the length of the room and Beth walking beside me in case I lose balance. After the warm-up, we are into it. Every fifteen seconds, Beth calls it. Jab. Jab. Left uppercut. Cross punch and uppercut. Knees and jabs. I love it. Getting into the zone. I feel alive, jabbing and ducking, my hair a mess, my muscles and biceps hardening, my tendons flexing. But most of all I love learning how to fight. For when the day comes. For the day he arrives on my doorstep. Because it will happen. And I will be ready.

Today I punch hard. To get it all out. I grit my teeth and grunt with every connection. I listen to Beth's instructions with laser focus. I try to knock her off balance. But she's too strong. Like a brick wall. Finally, she calls time a little before 7 p.m. so she can prepare for class.

35

"You're were a million miles away tonight," she says, putting the equipment back.

"Yeah."

She doesn't say anything else, like, do you want to talk about it? Or do you need a shoulder to cry on? That's not Beth's style. Her style is to be there if you need her. She's a woman of few words and I like it that way.

Women filter into the gym, ready for class.

"You did good today," she says, without looking back.

It's cold and dark by the time I leave the gym. It's always a downer when a session is over. You would think I would have a nice endorphin hit, and I do, but the reality of my life is a great leveler because inside the gym I can reach great heights but out here I am back to just being a cripple. It's like having a dream you can fly only to wake up and realize you can't.

The disclosure problem returns with a thud and all at once I'm weighed down and all my good gym work is out the window. Don't get distracted, I tell myself, get distracted and you'll make mistakes. Miss something that might be out of place, a person, a vehicle, and you'll be at risk. Think about the disclosure issue when you are safe at home.

I manage to cast it aside and advance along the pavement, taking a hard left, passing a fast food joint with a flickering old-school neon sign. I smell cooked hamburger meat and my stomach growls.

The sidewalk is unusually busy with people and I feel a little skip in my heart. Too many faces to scrutinize at once. I double my pace, but it's hard with the cane, and I'm soon short of breath. Forced to pause for a second, I hike my gym bag up my shoulder. Glancing behind me, I catch sight of a man a few yards back. A cold finger runs down my spine. His gait, the way he holds his shoulders, the straightness of his back, the baseball cap down low. Especially the baseball cap. It could be Him. Bending to pick up my bag, I dare to look again. He's paused now, studying the menu of a diner. Stalling? Waiting for me?

My every nerve ending screams. I need to leave. I need to leave now. I double my efforts and pick up speed, ignoring the shooting pain in my foot, trying to keep my cane from swinging out too wide so I won't accidentally fall flat on my face. I'm sure he's on the move again, even though I don't stop to look. I can sense him, eyes trained on the back of my head, walking up behind me to do Lord knows what.

Do not turn around, I tell myself, turn around and he'll know that you've clocked him.

I duck into an unfamiliar subway entrance. I know this is a mistake as soon as I do it because unfamiliar routes and deviations could mean blind alleyways and unexpected obstacles. Stupid me. Panic is taking over. I am losing control.

Thankfully there's nothing but a subway platform and a train about to depart. I race for it and my gym bag slips from my shoulder and falls to the ground. I leave it where it lands, breaking into a woeful half-jog, desperate to reach the train before it takes off, and I do, a millisecond before the doors close, narrowly avoiding catching my cane in the gap between the train and the platform.

Breathless, I look up through the dirty windows as the train rolls away. No one is there. Just my blue and gray gym bag on the platform, sitting there like a bomb about to explode.

8

In the beginning, after the incident, I used to see him all the time. Everywhere. In the grocery store, at the hospital, the courthouse, a face in a passing cab, my apartment building. I'd feel the terror of being choked all over again, the tightness around my throat, the suffocation of the dirt on top of my body. I had panic attacks on an almost daily basis. Lorna said it was natural and that with time it would pass. She said that the brain is remarkable and can't tell the difference between the real and the intensely imagined. That didn't help. If you can't tell the difference between what's real and what isn't, how are you ever supposed to know if someone is really following you or not?

I reach up to check the latch on the bedroom window. The morning sun is pushing its way through the glass. My watch alarm beeps. The 8 a.m. reminder. I have to get to court.

Satisfied the window is secure, I step back and the sleeve of my suit skims soot-colored dust from the window architrave. Cursing, I go to the bathroom and turn on the faucet to clean it off. I catch my face in the mirror, the lank hair, the dark circles under my eyes, the grim, downward pull of my mouth. It's been weeks since I've slept properly, and last night, after the scare, I couldn't stop myself from checking. I was like two selves, an observer and a crazy person, circling each other like dogs. Rather than stop at my normal three times, I checked four, then five times. I couldn't help myself. It was as if someone had taken over my body. I stunk from the gym and needed a shower and had to prepare for the next day at court. But on and on I went, checking the blinds, the locks on the doors, closet, and windows. Checking and checking and checking. So the call to Eileen Mercer about the disclosure issue never happened.

I think back to last night, to my gym bag on the platform, a symbol of my stupidity and weakness, and get angry all over again. Angry that I lost control and let irrational fear get the better of me.

I had barely managed to get home without completely falling to pieces. My purse was in that bag. My identification. Driver's license. Court credentials. A photograph of my face. Where I lived. I couldn't believe I had been so stupid. Keeping all that sensitive information in one place was a total rookie mistake. In my mind's eye, I could see him, crossing the platform, sweeping up the bag, retreating to some dark corner to rifle through its contents, grinning a big Bingo grin when he'd discovered he'd hit pay dirt on the whereabouts of Amelia Kellaway.

And that was my second mistake. I went home. I was so relieved to have my phone with my subway pass and apartment keys in my jacket pocket that I never thought through the implications of going back to the apartment. It wasn't until I opened my apartment door that I realized how dumb I had been. He could have beat me home. He could've been in the apartment, lying in wait.

But as I stood there frozen to the spot, heart smashing against my chest, I thought back to the man on the street. And the more I thought about him, the more unsure I became. Was it really him? Yes, the height and build were similar, but the posture was different, the coloring, his gait too. The man in the street was younger, more sprightly than a man in his early fifties. And he would be even older now, more worn down by life like I was. As I stood there, thinking, I was reminded of something Lorna had said: my memories had been distorted by trauma and time. Simply put, I couldn't trust my own eyes anymore. It probably wasn't him, just my overactive negative-bias imagination, superimposing his face on another person. And my bag? Well, whoever the lucky recipient was would probably be more concerned with the cash and credit cards than where I lived.

So I began to relax a little and made a few cautious steps into the apartment and that's when I saw it. My purse on the kitchen counter next to my work satchel. In the rush to get to the gym, I must have left it there. The relief was overwhelming, like a hundred-pound weight had been lifted off my shoulders. The only thing in that gym bag would have been a bottle of water, some tampons, a sweat towel, and a change of clothes.

But I still went mad with the checking, and now it's after 8 a.m. and I'm due in court and I'm so tired I can barely think. A tear leaks from my eye. I bat it away roughly. How did things get so out of control?

I put down the toilet seat lid and sit and hold my head in my hands. How am I going to make it through the hearing today? Maybe I should resign. Stay in my apartment all day. Stay here forever.

Then I think of Susie and the other little girls and the monster who thought he was so clever he was going to get away with what he'd done and then do it all over again.

I rise. No. It is up to me. There isn't anyone else who can do this. I rinse my sleeve in the basin and get ready to leave.

9

Courtrooms have a distinctive smell. Sweat and anxiety. The angst of the defendants, the witnesses, the victims, even the lawyers. It somehow leaches into the walls, embeds itself into the upholstery and fixtures. No one comes away clean, especially me.

I'm not a natural public speaker. I hate the way everyone stares when I talk, how they watch me limp across the courtroom to address a witness, how my voice shakes and makes me sound weak.

"Well, Ms. Kellaway?"

It's Judge Brown. An attractive woman in her mid-sixties with a severe brunette bob. Rumor has it, Judge Brown frequents S&M clubs after hours, but as far as I'm concerned, she's still a very capable judge and doesn't suffer fools gladly, although the biggest fool right now is probably me.

I look back at Judge Brown and remain rooted to my seat. I feel an emptiness in the pit of my stomach. I've had nothing to eat (I'm pretty sure black coffee doesn't count), and now I'm thinking that was a big mistake. I'm usually so good before a trial. My go-to is a simple eggs-over-easy on grainy toast, a nice protein/carb combo for sustained energy across the day. But this morning, even if I felt like eating, I didn't have time, and I can feel my blood sugar levels plummeting already.

Another thing is deodorant. Or more specifically, a lack thereof. In my haste, I forgot to apply my "shower fresh" Dove roll-on and now my nose is twitching at the offensiveness of my own rank body odor, made all the worse because today I seem to be sweating buckets beneath my sensible navy suit.

A stone's throw away is the defense table, and I wonder if Eileen Mercer can smell me too. She's certainly looking at me, left eyebrow arched high on her forehead, toying with the creamy string of lustrous pearls around her chubby neck. Close to seventy, the woman is still as sharp as a tack. Not a smidge over five-foot-one, she has the figure of someone who spends most of their day at their desk. Her rotundness works in her favor. That, combined with her seniority, somehow seems to add to her authority.

Next to her is the defendant, Alistair Kennedy, scribbling notes, rogue teacher, abuser of little girls. The picture of respectability in his nicely pressed whiter-than-white shirt and crimson polka dot tie. He could have been one of the lawyers and not the client. Behind him, the public gallery is full and restless. All eyes are on me. Expectant. Sitting in the second row from the front I spot Detective North in his crumpled shirt. He flashes me a frown of concern.

I get it. I'm concerned too. My peculiar set of neuroses is getting in the way of thinking straight, let alone doing my job.

This morning my intention had been to speak with Eileen Mercer before court and come clean about Susie's previous allegations. I had arrived at the conclusion that I would have to tell the truth and face the consequences and hope that the judge excluded the admission on the grounds it was historical.

But then I saw Susie in the corridor. Claire Watson had put a pink ribbon in her hair, which made her look more like nine than eleven and all the more vulnerable. I thought about what Susie had gone through, which was at least as bad as what I had experienced if not worse because of her age, and how courageous she was for wanting to confront the monster who took away her innocence.

Detective North was waiting with them. He'd stood when he saw me.

"You okay?" he'd asked.

"Fine. I'm fine. Just running a bit late."

I couldn't look him in the eye. I felt so duplicitous.

"I think they're waiting for you in there," he'd said.

I'd glanced through the window. Everyone was seated apart from the judge. According to the Lawyers Rules of Professional Conduct and Ethics my overriding duty was to the court, so it was clear what the proper course of action should be—go in there and call for a sidebar and inform the court of Susie's previous allegations and let the chips fall where they may.

But I didn't do that. Instead, I put on my game face and reached for the handle and entered the room and waited until Judge Brown took her seat. Then I delivered my opening and listened to Eileen Mercer deliver hers. I called the first of my two witnesses—the hospital medical examiner—and stepped her through her evidence, and took note of the jurors' appalled expressions when they saw the graphic nature of the diagrams. And then…well, then the time finally arrived, the point of no return, when I had to choose whether or not to call Susie as a witness or call a sidebar instead.

So here I am now, with Judge Brown looking at me over the top of her glasses with her penetrating gaze and the whole court is waiting and I know this is my very last

44

chance to act. I feel the weight of Eileen Mercer's stare. She knows. Everyone knows. I am playing with fire. I will get disbarred. I will cause a mistrial. Part of me is screaming for a sidebar. If I do it now the case could still be salvageable. My addled brain can't handle this mess. If only I had gotten some sleep. My lips go numb and I smell something, the stale air of the subway, and for one God awful minute I think I'm going to pass out, right there in the middle of the courtroom.

Eileen Mercer gets to her feet. "Really, Your Honor?"

"Indeed," says the judge, giving me a steely look. "Ms. Kellaway, either present your next witness or rest your case."

There's still time. I could still call for an adjournment. I could still make the disclosure. A murmur filters throughout the court. Everyone is waiting. I fight the urge to flee and never come back.

"Ms. Kellaway."

I rise to my feet. It's a miracle we've made it this far, to trial, after the tentative early days of the arraignment, the defense's pathetic attempts at a plea agreement in return for a suspended sentence, the eventual withdrawal of each witness, apart from one.

"Your Honor, I call Susan Angela Watson to the stand."

10

I look at poor Susie in the witness box. A smile forms on her lips. A kind smile for a kid. As if she can feel my terror and wants to reassure me that everything's going to be okay. Prior to Susie taking the stand, the witness screen had been wheeled into court. The lightweight laminate partition is effective in its simplicity, and completely obstructs any view that Susie has of Alistair Kennedy and him of her, although the jury, who are seated to Susie's left, can see her clearly, including, I hope, the same slightly trembling chin that I'm witnessing.

I take a breath and begin. We start with the easy questions first, her name, date of birth, where she attended school. Then we get into the evidence proper. The tough stuff. The kind of stuff that makes juries cringe. I steer her through her evidence-in-chief, one painful incident at a time. Four incidents, in particular, that mirror the charges brought against Kennedy. Susie confines herself to answering the questions, just as we talked about during her pre-trial prep, offering no more information than necessary. She does well, leaning into the microphone and speaking clearly so everyone can hear. A slight quiver thins her voice but she holds herself together in a way that is both admirable and heartwarming in its sincerity.

We get to the storeroom incident at the school involving the digital penetration and I hone in on the details. There are intakes of breath. People shift in their seats. It's unpleasant and hard to listen to but critical for everyone to hear. I look at the jury. Seven men. Five women. Three

Latino. One black. One Korean. One Lebanese. The rest white. A good cross-section overall. Two are crying.

"Susie, are you able to identify the man who did that to you?"

"Yes."

I enter in a large poster-sized six-person montage as Exhibit 12.

"Can you point him out in this montage labeled Exhibit 12?"

She raises her hand and points to Alistair Kennedy's face.

From his chair to the right, Kennedy shifts uncomfortably, his mouth a grim flat line. In the row directly behind him, his loyal wife and three grown sons are stone-faced in their seats.

"Susie, is what you've told us here today the truth?"

Her reaction is immediate. Shoulders back. Chin raised. She nods. "Yes, Ms. Kellaway, it is."

I turn to the judge. "Nothing further, Your Honor."

There's a short recess and then Susie is back on the stand. Eileen Mercer gets to her feet. I study the worn carpet in front of the witness box and begin to shake. This forty-plus-year veteran once worked for the same prosecution office as I did but turned her back on the public service for a career defending the indefensible. She was an idealist and believed everybody deserved a defense no matter what they were accused of. Mercer played by the rules and firmly expected that everyone else should too. If she ever found out that I had not disclosed something I should have, there would be hell to pay. A complaint to the Bar, the loss of my practicing license in the district of

New York, possibly the entire length of the United States. Mercer was a powerful woman in the legal profession and she would never let it go.

I had studied her as a law student, attending six of her trials. She was renowned for her cross-examination techniques. And she certainly had a talent, that was for sure, and could unravel witness testimony like no other lawyer I had ever encountered. One strand at a time, methodical, ruthless in her action but soft in her tone. She would peer at the jury over her glasses every time a witness faltered as if to say "see, he's not telling you the truth." She was a skilled operator and juries loved her sharp wit and her grandmotherly demeanor. Hiring her was the smartest thing Alistair Kennedy could have ever done.

"How are you, dear?" says Mercer, throwing a kindly smile Susie's way.

Susie pulls at her sleeve, "I'm good, ma'am. Thank you."

But Susie looks anything but good. Her evidence-in-chief has clearly drained her and I wish I had requested an adjournment until morning.

"I'm going to ask you a few questions, Susie, and then you can get down. Does that sound fair?"

"Yes, ma'am," Again, the tug of the sleeve.

Mercer takes the half-moon spectacles from around her neck and holds them up to read her notes.

"Susie," she says, letting her spectacles drop to her ample bosom, "Susie, do you know the difference between telling the truth and a lie?"

I go cold.

"Yes, ma'am."

Mercer pauses and gives the jury a meaningful look.

"We all tell fibs from time to time, Susie. But we're in a court now, in front of a judge. All of us must tell the truth here."

I feel the blood rise up my neck and into my face. I feel completely and utterly sick. Susie glances at me, uncertain. I look away.

"I know," says Susie, "I am."

Mercer draws close to the witness box, her Laura Ashley pumps slipping slightly against the gossamer of her hosed feet.

She lowers her voice and speaks gently. "When police questioned you at the start, you said Mr. Kennedy never touched you. Isn't that right?"

Susie nods. "He told me not to tell."

I let out a breath. That's it? That we can handle.

"Did you tell your mother?" continues Mercer.

"No."

"Your best friend? What is her name?" Mercer glances at her notes. "Emily?"

Susie starts to cry. "I'm not lying."

Mercer puts a box of tissues on the ledge in front of Susie. Lets her settle for a bit. She can't afford to alienate the jury and she knows it.

"It's all right, dear. Take your time."

Susie reaches for a tissue and wipes her eyes. She looks at the judge, cheeks blotchy from crying. "Can I go home now?"

Judge Brown offers her a sympathetic smile. "When you've answered all of Ms. Mercer's questions."

Still teary, Susie nods silently. My heart aches. But there's nothing I can do.

"There's been a lot of fighting at home, hasn't there, Susie? Your Mom and her new boyfriend haven't been getting along, have they?"

Susie looks at her knees.

"That must be hard."

Susie bites her lip. "Sometimes they shout."

"They split up, didn't they?"

Susie nods.

"And your Mom's been struggling to cope?"

"Mom's been sad."

"Isn't it the case, dear, that Mr. Kennedy simply gave you a hug when you got upset after what's been going on at home?"

Susie shakes her head. "No."

Mercer turns to the jury. "You've been distraught about it, haven't you? So distraught, in fact, that you felt you needed attention. A story like the one you've made up here would give you the attention you desired, wouldn't it, Susie?"

I get to my feet. "Objection, Your Honor, she's badgering the witness."

Mercer fakes outrage. "I resent that, Your Honor. These questions must be put to the witness. They are central to the defense's case and I am certainly not badgering the witness."

Judge Brown agrees. "Sustained."

I sit down and Mercer turns to Susie, whose eyes are locked on the tissue she's twisting in her hands.

"You're doing very well, dear. Almost there."

Susie sniffs and nods. Mercer pauses and frowns at the ceiling as if something has just occurred to her. It's an act. I know this because I've seen her do it before. It's called "taking the jury along on the journey" so they can feel like they are discovering "the truth" in real time right along with the defense. But a good lawyer never asks a question they don't already know the answer to and Mercer is a great deal better than just a good lawyer.

Mercer turns to look at me, a hint of a smile on her lips. "Susie, I'm wondering if you've made similar claims before?"

I stop breathing.

"Another teacher perhaps?" says Eileen Mercer, consulting her notes. "Back in Seattle, six, no seven, years ago?"

"I don't know," says Susie shakily.

Mercer frowns, overplaying her disappointment. "Come on now, dear, you know that's not true. Isn't it actually a fact that your mother told you to say that a preschool teacher, a Mr. Lucas Ackerman, sexually assaulted you? And didn't your mother insist that your preschool pay her a substantial sum of money to stop your allegation from reaching the police?"

I swing around and look at Claire Watson. She won't meet my eye.

"And isn't it true that your mother was eventually found out and charged with making a false complaint to police?"

I get to my feet. My cane clatters on the floor. "Objection!"

"I don't know," sobs Susie.

Mercer flaps a piece of paper in the air. "I have the police report right here, Your Honor."

"Objection!" I repeat. "The defense has failed to disclose this information. The prosecution has not had adequate time to consider it."

Mercer looks at me. "Oh, you really want to go down that road?"

Judge Brown bangs her gavel. "Overruled, Ms. Kellaway."

"But Your Honor!"

"I said overruled, Counselor. Take your seat."

I remain standing, my trembling hand perched on the edge of my desk.

"Now, Counselor, sit," says Judge Brown.

I concede and lower myself into my chair and watch helplessly as Mercer turns back to Susie and proceeds to tear her to shreds. "I put it to you, Susie, that Mr. Kennedy was only ever kind to you and that none of the events you outlined in your testimony ever took place."

Susie, sobbing loudly, swings her head back and forth. "No."

Mercer continues her attack. "I put it to you that you are a very confused little girl who has not told the truth here today, most likely cajoled and coached by your mother into making these outrageous claims against my client in pursuit of some material gain."

"No...please...I can't," chokes Susie.

I stand. "Objection, Your Honor! She's hounding the witness!"

"Momma!" wails Susie. "Momma!"

"Nothing further," says Mercer, resuming her seat.

11

I'm facing John Liber, my boss, the New York County District Attorney. Every time I see John, I think of Tony Soprano, dark-haired, larger-than-life, a diamond in the rough. He recently lost a ton of weight after a heart scare and his once plump jowls now hang deflated and fleshy around his neck, much like his shirts, which he has yet to update to a smaller size. John sits back in his chair and laces his hands over his belly. A mannerism that doesn't seem to carry quite the same consequence now that he's reduced so much of his girth.

"What the hell happened in there yesterday?" he says.

I don't answer. I don't know what to say.

He softens his voice. "You struggling, Am, is that it?"

He picks up the NutriBullet blender cup at his elbow and takes a chug of his thrice-daily Spirulina smoothie. I think back to the time, just over three years ago, when I approached John for this job. He knew my background, how damaged I was, and still took me on.

"You look like shit, kid," he says, draining the cup. "When was the last time you had a decent night's sleep?"

"I'm fine."

I look away. His office is a mess. Morning light seeps through the blinds, lowered for as long as I have known him, and stacks of files teeter preciously on top of his desk and litter the floor around it. John's a very busy man, with an entirely unmanageable workload, but he tries to keep across all the cases, which he does with varying degrees of success. He was the one who decided to go ahead with the

Kennedy prosecution even though all the other witnesses pulled out.

"Who in the hell do you think you're kidding? Anyone can see you're not coping."

I feel tears burn. I don't want to cry in front of him.

"It's not that bad," I say.

"Not that bad? Geeze, Am. You just caused a fucking mistrial."

The dreadful scene flashes into my mind. A distraught Claire Watson shouting profanities from the public gallery after Judge Brown granted Eileen Mercer's motion for a mistrial. A sobbing, almost hysterical, Susie wailing for her mother. A shell-shocked Detective North looking on as Claire struggled with two bailiffs as they escorted her from the courtroom. A clearly elated Alistair Kennedy pumping Eileen Mercer's hand and then pivoting to hug his wife and sons. Images, I knew, that would stay with me forever. His teaching license wouldn't even be revoked. The worst that would happen was in a few months the school board would quietly encourage him to move on and he'd continue his predatory ways in another school.

"It was an impossible choice," I say.

John stares at me in disbelief. "Choice? You didn't fucking have a choice. They're called rules. We're lawyers. We follow them. That simple."

"Not everything is so black and white."

He raises his eyebrows. "You really want to argue about this?"

I look at my hands. "I know I screwed up, John. Maybe we can relay charges. He wasn't acquitted."

I'm reaching and we both know it.

"That ain't gonna happen. I've already heard from the Bar Association. Mercer put in a complaint against you right away. I got no choice but to suspend you, kiddo, pending the outcome."

I'm shocked. "What? You can't do that."

"Just be grateful I'm not firing your ass. If it was anyone else…"

I bristle, "I don't need your pity, John."

"Am, come on. You're a great lawyer. I don't want to lose you. But you fucked up so you're out of here until the matter is resolved. With your impeccable record, hopefully you'll just get a censure, maybe a fine." His jaw clenches. "But with Mercer on your ass…we both know what a tough cookie she is. We need to play this by the book. A suspension shows the Bar we are taking the matter seriously, and Amelia, this *is* serious. The DA's office needs to be squeaky clean. I can't have a staff member playing by her own rules. What you did, well, it brings all of us into disrepute."

I lower my head and study my hands. "I said I was sorry, John. What about my other cases? Susie's was only one in a stack of a hundred, and there's an arraignment tomorrow for the liquor store holdup case."

"Already reassigned."

I feel like throwing up. Everything I care about is being taken away.

"Kiddo, I've been telling you to go on a vacation for months. Do it. Sort yourself out."

"I don't want to go on vacation."

John Liber pauses. "Lorna Stewart called."

I'm pissed. Whatever happened to doctor-patient confidentiality?

"She had no right to do that."

"We had a deal, Am. Every month. You promised you would go."

"I got busy, John."

"Three years, working night and day, you got burnt out. Your judgment was affected."

I sit there, unmoving. "I'm sorry, John."

He nods and lets out a sigh. "I know, kiddo. I know."

12

I'm on the train, homebound. My satchel empty of files. My heart heavy with failure. John Liber's disappointment stings. Part of me, that fragile little girl part of me, needs his approval and not having it hurts. Terrific, I tell myself, add being pathetic to the growing list of things wrong with me.

It's barely midmorning and the train car is almost empty. Just me and a teen with hot pink Dr. Dre headphones. Probably skipping school. I like the space. I feel safe here. I can breathe. I can almost convince myself I'm normal.

I consider staying on, zoning in and zoning out, and just riding. But I can't risk another blackout. And I'm bone-tired. I need sleep. If I don't get sleep, I won't be able to remain alert. If I don't remain alert, I'll make mistakes. If I make mistakes, I'll put my life at risk.

I elect to get off two stops early and take the long way home despite the fatigue. This is both a test of will and stamina, but there's also a practical reason. I need to compensate for my low bandwidth today. Being extra cautious will go some way to tipping the balance back in my favor.

Given the time of day, there are more people about on the streets than I would usually encounter during my weekday getting-home-after-work ritual. Shoppers. Pensioners. Facilities workers. When I arrive at the playground across from my apartment, it's busy with chatting mothers in puffer jackets and kids playing on swings. My pulse quickens. I can't do my usual checking because they'll be suspicious about what I'm up to. This change in sequence makes me nervous and I begin to sweat beneath my woolen coat.

Swallowing down anxiety, I pass through the playground, avoiding running children in case they trip over my cane. I stop when I reach the other side of the street. The only thing I can think of is to pull out my phone and make it look like I'm checking Google Maps for directions. No one pays me any attention so I hold the phone higher, until my apartment block is in my eyeline. I commence the checking process, sweeping left to right, studying each balcony and, finally, my own. Everything looks okay. The blinds look the same. But I make myself check again because I know I'm tired and I don't want to risk missing anything.

When I'm done, I tell myself to move on or the mothers will start to worry. I clap up the pavement toward my building and go inside, closing and locking the shared front door, taking the archaic elevator up to my floor, wrangling with the dead bolts and retreating inside. Once there, I pause to lay down my satchel and turn on the heat. Then I begin checking.

The apartment seems strange in daylight. Noises are different. Objects too. There seems to be more of them. The furniture looks like it belongs to someone else.

It throws me off balance. I tell myself it's okay, just trust the process because I know the process works well. It is painstaking in its thoroughness and will catch anything amiss. So that's what I do, checking the living room, the windows, the kitchen, the bathroom, the spare room door, my bedroom, the closet, and so on.

I'm so sore. Everything hurts. My eyeballs, hair, skin. My bladder is screaming for relief. But I need to finish checking first.

I'm in my bedroom when my phone rings in my pocket. I nearly jump out of my skin. I check it and see my mother's number. I wonder if she's had a call from John Liber. Would he go that far? Would he really call my mother?

I let it pass to voicemail and try not to get angry with John or my mom, which will only cloud the quality of my checking, and return to the process. I pause and look at my bedroom window. Did I check that already? I think I did but now I can't remember. The phone call has interrupted my flow and now I have lost my place and I'm out of sequence. I will have to start again. Tears spill over. God. Damn. It.

I tell myself to stop being such a crybaby, stop being so goddamn weak. I brush the tears away and start again, trudging through the apartment, my foot throbbing, head aching.

When I'm finally done, I return to the bathroom and put the plug in the tub and turn on the faucet. I sit on the edge of the bath, waiting for it to fill, staring into the middle-distance fog.

A hazy memory of the last time I took a bath in the daytime comes to me. I was ten and had tonsillitis and my mother made me an egg sandwich on soft white bread laden with butter. Life was so simple back then. When the bath is drawn, I slip into the warm bubbleless water, too aware of my own nakedness in the daylight. There's also the ugly half foot bobbing at the end of the tub, demanding I pay attention, whether I want to or not. I wash myself quickly, get out, dry off, and climb into bed.

I lie there. Count the squares on the wallpaper. Trying to ignore the light leaching through the shades. I lie there for hours. Until there are after-five noises of people arriving home from work, climbing the stairs, turning on their heat, feeding their cats and themselves. Even though it's not exactly sleeping, I'm not moving and that's something. I tell myself to drift, let go, that eventually slumber will come.

There's a knock on the front door. My heart flips. I hold my breath, straining to hear. Another knock. Who could it be? What do they want? This has never happened before and I don't know what to do. I lie as still as I can. Hoping that whoever it is will not hear the drumbeat of my heart. Another knock. Louder this time. Go away, just please go away. I wait, but there's nothing more. Maybe they're gone.

I get out of bed, pull on my robe, and go check. In the living room the blinds are open even though it's dark out by now. Then I see him, walking away, up the street, Detective Ethan North. I hang back and watch him. His weary gait, hands in his pockets, collar up around his neck.

I have the awful, fleeting thought that something bad has happened to Susie. I should call him. I reach for my satchel, find his card, pick up my cell. I hesitate. If I call, he will know I was here all the time. I color at the thought. My craziness on display for him to see. No, I don't want that. I want to salvage what little dignity I have left. Besides, there's nothing I can do for Susie in the state I'm in right now. I can barely take care of myself.

I look out the window again. He rounds the corner and disappears from view and I feel an overwhelming sense of relief. I close the blinds completely and shut off the lights, then return to my bed. Sleep is never going to come now so I might as well do something useful. I take the key from the trinket box next to my bed and return to the hallway. Facing the spare room door, I unlock it and go inside.

13

I wake up on my bedroom floor. This hasn't happened to me for over a year. This strange form of sleeping walking, when I somehow go from being in the spare room to the middle of my bedroom floor. It's like my mind has some perverse need to recreate the trauma of being lost in the woods, to reinvent that hard, unforgiving forest ground. As if my body is addicted to the pain and can't let go.

I stretch for the trinket box and look inside. The spare room key is in there. I must have returned the key in the night, although I don't remember doing so. My chest tightens. I don't like this, this awful sense of confusion and gaps in time.

I sit up and a groan escapes my lips. My left hip aches and so does my back. But at least I slept. That's something.

I check my phone for the time. 9:07 a.m. Another missed call and a text from Lorna. *I'm free at ten. Come see me.* I get up and make coffee.

*

Lorna doesn't know what I'm thinking. I tell myself this as she nods and listens to my lies.

"The band is working." I raise my wrist and ping the stupid rubber band.

"Oh good."

"I snap right out of the spiral."

I've come to know Lorna well. The little tug at the corner of her mouth like she's tasted something bad. She gets it whenever I talk about him, like she's personally offended he ever walked the face of the earth. I know every inch of her office, too. The bookcase. The oriental doorknocker behind the glass frame. The Jo Malone Pomegranate Noir scent diffuser on top of the little table to the left.

Lorna thinks that because there are no photos on display the office is impersonal, but it's not. There are telling details everywhere. For instance, her favorite color is teal. It's in the carpet, the curtains, even the flowers on her coffee cup are teal. She drinks loose-leaf Japanese Lime tea, not coffee, so I'm guessing she takes care of her health. She's orderly, almost compulsively so. The titles of her books are organized alphabetically, spine out, not a speck of dust in sight. And she has been a traveler in the past. I know this because she once told me that the gray-blue Persian rug in the center of the room came from a trip to Istanbul when she was in her twenties.

But there are things I don't know, like whether she has kids or not. She holds herself like a single woman but my intuition is a little off these days, so I could be wrong. There's a sadness about her, too. She's seen pain. I recognize it. I once saw her in the street. She never saw me. She never looked up. She was frowning at her phone with a disappointed look on her face. I felt the urge to follow her. I wanted to see where she went, who she met. But I stopped myself and just let her walk by.

"And the work situation?" she says.

Ah, so John Liber told her.

"I'm over it."

"Really?"

"No."

"Okay."

I look at my hands, twirl the band around my wrist. I should tell her. All of it. My feelings. How everything is getting worse. How I'm losing control. That I need help.

I look up. "The son of a bitch, Kennedy, is going to get away with it now."

"You're angry."

"Of course."

"At who, Amelia? Yourself?"

I shrug. "Yes."

She reaches for the mug with the teal flowers and takes a sip. "You're holding back."

"My life's in limbo. I could get disbarred."

"You don't like the feeling of loss of control."

"Would you?"

She winces.

"God, I'm sorry, Lorna," I say. "I don't mean to snap."

She holds up a hand. "It's fine."

I hesitate. "I thought I saw him."

"Rex Hawkins?"

I nod.

"When?"

"Yesterday. In the street. It wasn't him though."

She presses me. "You panicked."

I nod. "Yeah."

"Anything else?"

I remain silent.

"The checking? How's that been?"

I shrug. "The usual."

"Amelia."

I feel tears but manage to hold them back.

Lorna changes tack. "Tell me about when you thought you saw him."

"I was leaving the gym. It felt like someone was following me. He was the same build."

"Did you see his face?"

"He had a cap on. It was the way he walked. It was the same way as he did. That's what I thought anyway."

"What happened?"

"I ran." I look at my foot. "Well, whatever it is I do now since becoming a cripple. I made it to the train and when I turned around, he was gone."

"So no one was following you after all? Let alone Rex Hawkins."

I pause.

"Amelia?"

I shrug. "I don't know."

"I see."

"Okay, no. It was my overactive imagination. Again."

"Do you still look at his photo on the internet?"

Suddenly I feel ashamed. "I don't know why I do that. I want nothing more than to forget him."

"It's the payoff. By doing it you're keeping him real, keeping the trauma alive. It helps you recall the color of his eyes, the texture of his skin, the way he smelled."

"You make him sound like a lover, that I'm getting some sort of fix by seeing his face."

She nods. "The compulsion is similar. Part of you is getting something from remembering him and not letting go. You're driven to set yourself up to be revictimized over and over again. It usually happens to children under the age of three who've been abused. The physiological arousal and stress responses they experience as infants can make them noradrenaline pain addicts later in life. But it can happen in serious trauma events in adults, and the worse cases of PTSD, too."

"So, basically, I'm bat shit crazy."

"I prefer the term 'work in progress.' The challenge for you is that this constant engagement with him—the thinking about him, looking at photographs, is keeping him alive in your mind. There is no difference between the real—"

"And the intensely imagined. I get it."

She pauses. "The checking is getting worse too, isn't it?" I must look surprised because she says, "It's all linked. There's a knock-on effect." She closes her notebook. "I think that should be your priority for the week—refraining from looking at his image. Once we get that under control, once he is less real to you, the need for obsessive checking ought to dissipate. Also, try reminding yourself how long it's been since the incident, and that you've been safe all this time. Use this downtime to work on yourself, Amelia. Maybe have a change of scene. Go see your mother. It's all about interrupting patterns."

*

What Lorna doesn't know is that I can't stop. It's not like I haven't tried, I have. But the compulsion to look is just too strong. I do it at least twelve times a day. There's an image of him on my phone, within easy reach. And private. There are other photos of him on the web taken prior to the incident with me, before he went into hiding. Him attending various philanthropic endeavors. Him in a feature article that included a photo of him on his ranch posing with his prize black Angus bull. Him surrounded by his oil refinery employees. But the one on my phone is my preferred photo. It's most like the friendly face I saw

66

that first day in the gas station. A head and shoulders shot of him on a horse looking straight into the camera. An easygoing, smiling good ol' boy. Skin slightly pinked from the sun. Happy to lend a hand. Or ask a naïve young woman for help.

Instead of trying to resist, I just give in. And look. Over and over. Each and every day. I look closely. Count the crow's feet, the inflection in his smile, the sharp line of the pressed collar of his plaid shirt, the steel behind his eyes. I look because it takes me back to the day in the gas station when he tricked me into helping him with the tire, then shoved me into the trunk of his car. How many times had he practiced that moonboot routine before he used it on me? I look until the initial shock of seeing his face passes and I feel nothing. I look because I don't want to forget. I can't afford to forget. One day it could be a matter of life and death.

14

After leaving Lorna's office, it's a toss-up between taking the ferry or the subway to get to New Jersey. Today the wind is cold and the Hudson is choppy, so I opt for the train. I have not been to Claire Watson's apartment before. In fact, I haven't been anywhere near New Jersey for years. Since returning to New York after the incident, I have confined myself to the city because venturing further afield makes me nervous.

I slip into Starbucks and order a large flat white and take a corner seat down the back. Before I go, I need to ensure my journey is mapped out thoroughly. Unfamiliarity could lead to errors. I need all my focus to be on the people and faces around me and not the street signs.

Using my phone, I search online for the best and safest routes, which trains to catch, what streets to walk down, the landmarks to look out for, the points where I will double back to cover my tracks. I study satellite images over and over until the New Jersey street patterns are clear in my head, taking a virtual journey from Point A to Point B to Point C then back to Point A again. It's a lot to keep organized, which is why I take my time, and only finish when I'm sure I can recall my plan without the prompt of my phone.

While a plan is a critical and very necessary thing, I recognize the reality that this virtual online roaming can never be foolproof. I will undoubtedly encounter unforeseen risks. Unidentified blind alleys, road work, building maintenance, blocked accessways. There will be times I will have to improvise. To help prepare for that possibility, I download maps, screenshots, and train schedules so I have them in easy reach. Only then do I feel satisfied that I have done enough to leave.

*

It takes me two and a half hours to travel from lower Manhattan to Newark, New Jersey. It would take a normal person, driving a normal car, just under an hour. But finally I'm here, standing in front of Claire Watson's grim-looking brown-brick rental complex. A monolith square with small windows and no balconies, the complex looks more like some sort of institution than a place where people make homes.

The elevator is broken, so I'm forced to take the stairs. Four flights in total. As I make my way upward, I try to ignore the putrid stench of urine and alcohol and possibly a dead rodent, and distract myself with the poorly executed graffiti covering the pockmarked plaster walls.

I had no idea that Claire and Susie lived in these conditions, and it makes me appreciate just how devastating the turn of events has been for them. No wonder Claire had been so desperate to set Susie on another path in life.

I locate Claire's apartment and knock. A minute later there's a rattle of locks and the door opens.

Claire stares at me. "I wasn't expecting anyone."

She looks rough, like she hasn't slept in days. Her unbrushed hair hangs in two knotty tails, one on each shoulder. The gray T-shirt she's wearing has a stain on the front. I begin to question the wisdom of coming.

For a moment, I think Claire's not going to let me in, but then she turns, leaving the door open, and I follow her up the hallway into the small living room. She sits down on a ripped black leatherette armchair and lights a cigarette.

"I didn't know you smoked."

She shrugs.

"How are you doing?" I ask, trying not to stare at the ashtray piled high with butts.

"Dandy."

"Claire."

"Amelia."

I pause, try to lighten my tone. "And Susie? How's she?"

"Last week she started a new school. Let's hope there are no leeches there. I wanted to keep her home, but I had a visit from Child Social Services. Can you believe that? Like I'm the one that needs monitoring. Fucking ridiculous," she says, tapping the ashtray. "They said she needed to be in school. I told them she was safer at home. But what do I know, I'm just her mother."

I wonder if she's on something, prescription medication or otherwise.

Suddenly, she looks at me, hopeful. "Are they going to re-lay the charges against Kennedy?"

I shake my head. "No."

"Well, you've got to convince them."

"I tried, but I'm not exactly flavor of the month."

"Try harder."

"I've been suspended."

She clucks her tongue and looks disgusted. "Figures."

I glance around the apartment. There's a pile of unfolded laundry on the sofa and the floor looks like it hasn't seen a vacuum in weeks.

"How are you doing, Claire? Really?"

She sucks hard on her cigarette. "My son-of-a-bitch boyfriend finally left me for good."

Her eyes land on a photo on the wall. A family portrait taken when Susie was an infant. "Get this. He said he couldn't cope with what happened. As if he was the one who was fingered by some creep in a dark room. Prick."

I take a breath. "I know this has been difficult, but the best thing you can do for Susie is pick up the pieces and move on."

"You have no idea what you're talking about."

My cell chimes with a text but I ignore it.

"Come on, Claire. Don't give up, Susie needs you."

She shoots me a bitter look. "Look around you. This is her future. It's never gonna get any better than this."

"Claire."

"I think you'd better go now."

I pause. "If that's what you want."

I get to my feet and head for the door. Claire doesn't move from her seat.

"And Amelia?" I turn and look at her. "Don't come back here again."

15

When I was eight, I was bitten by a spider. It crawled into the sleeve of my nightgown and up my arm and bit me on my collarbone while I slept. I showed my mother the next day.

"How do you know it was a spider?" she said.

"I just do."

"Did you see it?"

"No."

"Well, then," she said, turning back to peeling the potatoes, "you don't really know what it was."

I told my sister and brother and they didn't believe me either.

"It's probably a mosquito or something," said my sister. My brother just laughed.

That night I tore my room apart looking for it, shook out my sheets and blankets, removed my pillowcases, pulled my bed away from the wall, got down on all fours and examined the carpet. I couldn't find anything.

I hauled out the vacuum cleaner and cleaned around my bed, then emptied an entire can of bug spray all over my room. Even so, I was too afraid to sleep. It was going to come in the night and bite me again. I was sure of it.

The next day the bite, which began as a tiny pimple, had spread to the size of a nipple. A giant distinct circle just like an areola and a hard nub in the center. Within two days, it had formed puss and I got an infection. My mother took me to the doctor and he put me on a course of a high dose of antibiotics.

I looked for that spider for days. I looked even though my sister rolled her eyes and my brother teased me and my mother said I had a wild imagination.

A week later I was better and the bite went down and I began to forget about the spider. Then one day when I was getting ready for school, I went to put on my sneakers and there it was, in the toe of my shoe. Dead and big and brown, legs folded up on itself. A brown recluse spider. So it turned out I had been right all along.

As I study my apartment building from my usual place in the park across the road, I think about the spider. The spider that no one believed had existed except for me. I know Lorna thinks I'm just another one of her crazy paranoid patients. But I know he's out here, watching, waiting, biding his time. I'm not going to be his victim again. I'm not going to be another one of those sitting ducks that ends up being stabbed to death on her doorstep.

I spend a few minutes longer in the park. A couple in the upstairs apartment are intertwined, sharing a cigarette, gazing out the window. The man reaches down and kisses the woman's cheek then looks back out the window.

I cross the road and go inside my building. My foot aches badly so it's a relief when I get to the elevator and reach my floor.

When the lift door opens, I see a dark figure at the top of the stairs and scream. Before I know it, I'm running in blind panic, careening toward my apartment, dropping my cane and keys in the rush. All I can think of is he's here. He's going to kill me. I've got to get inside. I trip. Go down hard. Put my arms out to break my fall, slicing open my palm as I land on my keyring.

"Jesus, Ms. Kellaway are you okay?"

It takes a moment to register the voice. Ethan North.

I stay on the ground, shaking, unable to speak.

"Hey, it's okay," he says, reaching out to touch me.

I flinch and he backs off.

"You shouldn't sneak up on people like that," I say, my voice shaking.

"I wanted to make sure you were okay after the trial." He sees the cut on my hand. "Oh, you're bleeding."

The charm attached to the keyring, a little glass sphere containing a single fleecy dandelion seed, lies smashed on the floor. Blood is dripping down my arm.

"I'm fine."

"Let's get you inside."

Before I can stop him, he picks up my keys and unlocks the door. If he notices anything unusual about the number of locks, he doesn't say anything.

"Where's the bathroom?"

I gesture with my chin and he leads me through the apartment to my bathroom. Heading for the basin, he turns on the tap, angles my hand under the running water. The wound is nasty and gushing blood.

"We should get you to the emergency room. You might need stiches."

"It's just a cut."

He looks at the wound, frowning. "I think I see glass. Have you got some tweezers?"

I nod at the top drawer and he opens it. My medication and ointments for my foot are in there, a few stray tampons, and I suddenly feel very exposed. He finds the tweezers.

"Keep still," he says.

74

It hurts. I gasp.

"Sorry."

He digs a little more, then holds up a slither of glass. "Eureka."

"Eureka? Who says that anymore?"

He smiles. "My pop. I guess I get it from him."

He bandages the wound and looks at me when he's done. "How you doing? Better?"

I nod. "Yeah, thanks."

I suddenly become aware of how close he is. I stand up.

"I suppose a coffee's in order," I say.

*

We sit at the kitchen table, cradling our mugs.

"How did you know where I live anyway?"

He looks away and studies the baseboards. "I'm a cop."

"You didn't need to check up on me."

"That was a shitty thing what happened," he says. "You know, at court."

"It was my fault. I should have known better."

He's polite enough not to agree and looks over his shoulder to take in the apartment. "I came by the other night."

I feign surprise. "Oh, what night was that?"

He looks into his mug, takes a mouthful. "Tuesday."

I scramble for something convincing to say. "I think I was out."

He nods. His eyes land on the bottom shelf of the bookcase, the entire row that is dedicated to PTSD books. *The Body Keeps Score. Trauma and Recovery. The Complex PTSD Workbook. I Can't Get Over It: A Guide for Survivors of Trauma.* I wonder if he has questions. He must know what happened to me. Everybody does. But I don't feel like exposing my soul tonight.

His phone bleeps. He glances at it. "Just my pop."

"He lives with you?"

Ethan shakes his head. "He's in a home. He has Alzheimers."

"Oh, I'm sorry."

"He likes to text me the results of the game."

I get to my feet, tip out what's left of my coffee in the sink.

"You're tired," he says, standing.

"A bit."

He places his empty mug on the counter. "I'll let you get some rest." He pauses at the door, frowns a little. "You sure you'll be all right on your own?"

I nod. "I'm fine."

"All right then, enjoy your night."

He leaves before I remember to thank him.

16

My throbbing hand wakes me. At first, I'm confused. Then I remember. Ethan North. The graceless, face-first plunge to the floor. My neurosis on display for all to see. He had been kind. Warm. Tender, even. I think about the scar on his top lip, the dark full eyebrows framing his hazel eyes, the stubble just beginning to show. The maleness I should turn away from and be afraid of. But here, in the quiet of my bedroom, it doesn't seem so reckless.

There had been other men since the incident. Two to be precise. One of them was a fellow patient at the center, who had lost his arm in a wheat thrasher. The other was a Tinder date, a butcher from Queens. Not much more than fumbles in the dark, where I could be invisible and pretend to be someone else. I endured the encounters like some sort of punishment, coldly daring myself to feel the touch of a man and not have it matter. Part of me was worried that I might have a meltdown and think of the rape. As it turned out, I didn't because I only felt numb.

My hand throbs some more, demanding I get up and feed it ibuprofen. I reach for my phone to check the time and see two texts. The first is a reminder from Beth about the get-together at her place tonight. A celebration to mark her recent marriage to Gwen, a woman I had never met but suspected was the person in the party-driving seat given Beth, a textbook introvert, would rather be alone in the gym doing push-ups. I click on the second text and read it. I sit up, gripped by a sudden rush of hope.

*

I don't usually go to Chris's apartment in person but her text had been insistent. I have only been there once before, the first time we made the agreement; since then communication has been by email and text only.

"Safer for everyone that way," Chris had said.

At the time, I wasn't exactly sure what she'd meant, but I had accepted her terms. I was just glad to have finally found someone to help.

Chris and I first met at the gym. Chris was an old girlfriend of Beth's. A former Marine, complete with buzz cut and frank green eyes. When I asked her exactly what she had done in the Marines, she was evasive. "Intelligence," she had said cryptically and left it at that. It was only later that I found out from Beth that Chris had been a security analyst with links to the National Security Agency. She had tracked and investigated suspected terrorists and had access to databases and surveillance tools I could only dream of. After Chris left the Marines, she'd set herself up as a "consultant" doing "off the book" jobs. That was when I realized that maybe Chris could help me.

By the time I reach her apartment, it's just after 10 a.m. Located in a converted shoe factory down a dead-end street in Williamsburg, Brooklyn, the place is perfectly suited to Chris, nondescript and quiet and not easily found. Chris buzzes me in right away and I'm hit with the earthy smell of female perspiration.

"Hey," she says, breathing heavily.

Despite the chill, she's wearing a black wife-beater, camo shorts, no shoes. A sheen of sweat covers her bare skin and a pair of boxing gloves dangle from her hand.

"I took a little longer than I expected. Sorry," I say.

She tips her wrist to look at her chunky, multifunction sports watch but doesn't say anything. I wonder what event she is training for now. In addition to being a tech genius, Chris is a pain junkie hooked on Sufferfest and Spartan endurance events that would come close to killing any normal human being. Beth told me that Chris once ran for twenty-four hours straight with a torn Achilles tendon, and that after some crazy three-day challenge involving rope swings, barbed wire, and a thirty-mile run, Chris came home black and blue with bruises after plummeting forty meters down a sheer cliff face.

I look around. The place is exactly how I remember, essentially a large square room divided into four distinct areas. A kitchenette and adjoining bathroom. A combined sleeping and living area. A workout area complete with rowing machine, treadmill, red leather boxing bag, and stack of kettle bells. And, finally, an office space, heavy on the latest tech, complete with a high-end black leather office chair, multiple high-definition monitors, and every ergonomic accessory known to womankind.

I follow Chris across the room to the center of operations. She takes her seat and offers me an upturned wastepaper basket to sit on.

"It's okay. I'll stand."

I want to ask her what the urgency is about, but have learned that talking isn't really Chris's thing. I look over her shoulder and study the monitors, drawing breath when I see what's on the middle one. A super-clear high-definition satellite image of his compound. Neglected and overgrown. Fences chained up and padlocked. Thousands of oil drums stacked in an empty field.

Chris's slender fingers fly over the keyboard like some sort of tech Chopin as she works her magic on encrypted folders and subfolders.

Finally, I can stand it no longer. "What are we doing here, Chris? Did you find something?"

"*Un momento*," she says, frowning.

Several more keystrokes and a PDF document springs open.

"Take a look at that," she says, sitting back.

I lean in close even though the monitor is at least thirty-two inches. My pulse quickens. I study the image on the PDF. A poor-quality photocopy of a Portuguese driver's license. Same build and age.

I shake my head. "It's not him."

"Sure?"

I sigh, disappointed. "Yeah."

Chris looks at me. "I can't do this anymore."

"What do you mean?"

"I got a job, a real one. I need to go legit. Mainstream. I want kids one day."

"Kids?"

She nods, takes a chug from a water bottle. I feel discouraged. There's no way I can locate him on my own.

"Can you help me find someone else who can do the same thing as you?"

She pauses. "Isn't it about time you gave up? This guy. He's a ghost. He could be dead. Heart attack, whatever."

I shake my head. "He's out there somewhere."

"How can you be so sure?"

Twelve months Chris has been working on this. Twelve months and nothing. There is no Rex Hawkins as far as Chris is concerned. Maybe she's right.

"Just find me someone else," I say, heading for the door.

17

Not long after I leave Chris's apartment, my phone rings. I look at the screen. Mom. Again. I think about letting it go to voicemail. I don't want to talk about vacations to Bali. The pathetic state of my love life. Or how my career is in tatters. Oh, she means well, she really does, but talking to her is a reminder of what I once was, what I could have been. It's like a fall from grace from which I'll never recover.

My thumb hovers over Ignore. I suddenly feel racked with guilt. I can't keep avoiding her, because she'll think she's done something wrong when it's really not her, it's me. Me and my inability to heal and move on from the past.

I duck into a doorway and hit the answer button.

"Hiya, hon." I hear running water. I picture her at the sink washing dishes, phone wedged between her shoulder and ear. "You got my messages, then, about the vacation?"

"I did. Thanks." I pause. "How is everyone?"

"Your brother and sister? Why good, hon. What about you?"

"I'm fine, Mom."

I hear the tap twist off, the snap of latex as she removes her kitchen gloves. "You sure? You sound a bit flat."

"Did my boss call you?"

"Your boss? No. Why would he do that?"

"Never mind."

"Is something wrong, honey?"

"I'm fine, Mom. Really, I am. I'm sorry I haven't gotten back to you. I know it's been a while."

"Why don't you come visit on the weekend? We could go to brunch and visit one of the farmer's markets, get some fresh fruit for you to take home."

"That sounds nice, Mom. But I can't. You know, it's nuts here. Work."

"Oh sure." There's a pause. "It's just that I worry, Amelia."

My eyes mist. "I know, Mom."

We lapse into silence.

"Listen, I better go," I say.

"I understand, hon. It was lovely to talk to you."

"I'll call you."

"Oh, I almost forgot. Something came for you. A letter."

My mouth goes dry. "Oh?"

There's a rustle from her end. "Well, the things is, I opened it. By accident, of course. I didn't read who it was addressed to so I just assumed it was for me."

"Who was it from, Mom? What did it say?"

She lets out a breath. "That's the funny thing, sweets. The darn thing was empty."

*

In some ways an empty envelope is worse than a horse's head in your bed. It seems more sinister. More personal. More of a power play. See, I don't have to do much to terrorize you. Just send you an empty envelope and your fragile little mind will do the rest. And, of course, there's the implied threat. I know where your mom lives. I can get to her anytime I want.

I resist the urge to tell my mother to change the locks on her windows and doors. To move to a different town. Get a guard dog and some security surveillance. I don't want to scare her. I don't want her life to become the same as mine.

There's no evidence the empty envelope is from him, of course. But there's no return address, so it's unlikely to be an innocent mistake. I tell my mother to seal the envelope in a plastic bag and send it to my work address. I need to think about whether I want to take it further, have it analyzed for DNA, for clues as to where it was posted from. She's gracious enough to not ask too many questions.

I never told her but in the early days, in that first year after I had come back, there had been flowers. Tulips, red, always in a bundle of three, tied together with a thin black ribbon and left on my apartment doorstep. Another time there were pine cones, four, delivered one at a time over the course of a month. Hard, solid, and green, the brown woody scales yet to open up and spread, like the young pine cones I had encountered when I was lost in the wilderness.

The police looked into it and concluded it was probably a hoax. Most likely some sicko who'd read the papers playing mind games with me. I changed apartments and the tulips and the pine cones ceased and I began to think that maybe the police had been right after all.

And now the non-letter. That and the hang-up phone calls. It gives me the chills.

The incident pushes me into paranoia overdrive so the journey back home ends up taking over three hours. When I finally reach my usual lookout point at the park across the road from my apartment, my half foot throbs like crazy. My special sock feels sodden, too. I suspect blood.

That sometimes happens when I have been walking too much. There's likely to be a tear along the right side of the seam where the skin was surgically rejoined. It had occurred before, not long after the amputation, when my flesh refused to knit together. That time I'd been hospitalized and needed antibiotics intravenously for three straight days.

This time around I suspect the cause is my shoe. Because no matter how many times they redid the orthopedic insole, it rubbed along that strangely shaped section of my foot.

Even with the pain of my half foot, I don't move from the park to my apartment for another hour. It's only when one of the young mothers comes over to ask me if I'm all right do I finally move on. Everything is fine in my apartment. No break-ins. No sign that anyone has been there. At last I can relax.

Then I remember Beth's party tonight. I promised I'd be there. But going to a party is the last thing I feel like doing. I could make an excuse. A headache. Another commitment I'd forgotten about. Or simply not show in the hope I'm not missed.

But that's so unfair, not to mention rude. It's important that I be there for Beth like she's been there for me, so I decide I will go after all, stay for an hour and then quietly slip away.

I check the time. Three hours before the party starts. A nap might help restore some of my energy. So that's what I do, downing a couple of tramadol for my aching foot, not bothering to remove my clothes, or shoes for that matter, choosing instead to crawl into bed as is, pulling up the covers right up over my head.

18

I pull the brush through my hair, then pick up the tube of Maybelline light coral Color Sensation lipstick I found in the old makeup bag buried in the back of the bathroom cupboard. I run it over my lips and stand back to study my reflection. I'm not used to the makeup and feel tawdry.

I dab a little more concealer under my eyes, hoping to hide my exhaustion, then turn my attention to the pile of clothes on my bed. After an earlier sort through my spartan wardrobe it became plainly obvious I had nothing suitable to wear for a party. Anything close to festive or sparkly has long since been sent to Goodwill. I look at the pile and tell myself to just make a choice. I'm going to be late enough as it is. Eventually, I settle on a pair of jeans, white T-shirt, and blue blazer and pray it will be dark.

On the way out, I catch my reflection in the mirror. The makeup looks worse than I thought. I could be a carnival clown in a travelling circus so I go to the bathroom and wash it all off.

It's late by the time I reach the Tribeca address Beth gave me. It's a two-story, white-bricked loft with an art gallery downstairs and apartment on top. It looks expensive and not quite where I pictured Beth to be living, but then I recall her mentioning that her new bride, Gwen, is involved in the art world. Apparently, the art world pays particularly well.

From the street, I tilt my head to take in the apartment. The party's in full swing. Chatter, clinking glasses, and music, an old-school Britney Spears song, filter out across the otherwise quiet neighborhood. People are gathered behind large wall-sized windows or dancing outside under a string of colored lights on the rooftop terrace.

I want to turn around and go home. I don't even know these people. Harden up, I tell myself, this is a special and important occasion for Beth and it was nice she even thought to invite me. I should be grateful to have friends like her.

I buzz the security intercom next to the large stainless-steel door that looks like it may have once belonged to a meat processing factory. A few seconds later, the door clicks open and a disembodied voice tells me to take the stairs up to the second floor.

When I go inside, I'm surprised to see jet black walls and a grand, ultra-modern white lacquer staircase lined with flickering tealight candles. It looks beautiful but treacherous for someone with a cane. I proceed with caution, taking care that my cane doesn't slip on the highly polished surface.

When I reach the open door at the top, I see that the distinctive monochrome theme has been carried throughout the entire apartment. Black and white everything. Décor. Furniture. Even the art on the walls.

The apartment is an open plan concept and has a spacious, almost cavernous feel. A large living area flows into a super sleek kitchen, the roof-top terraced garden beyond that. The living area is populated with angular and very uncomfortable-looking designer furniture, offset with soft lighting and more candles. A large Jackson-Pollock-like canvas adorns the rear wall.

Beautiful people are mingling. Champagne glasses in hand, voices raised over the thumping music. None of the crowd look much like Beth's cup of tea, although I do recognize two of the Thursday night gym-goers talking over by the bar. I spot Beth on the patio, looking out of place in this glamorous setting. There's a woman by her side. Taller. Blonde. At least twenty years older than Beth. Dressed in flowing designer slacks and a sheer white chiffon blouse.

Beth is gazing at her new wife in adoration. I'm not sure I like it. I have always thought of Beth as the strong one. I approach them, ignoring the eyes dropping to my cane as I navigate my way through the crowd.

"Sorry I'm late," I say when I reach her.

"Hey, Amelia," says Beth, breaking into a smile. "Gwen, this is my friend from the gym, Amelia Kellaway."

Gwen gives me the once-over and extends a sinewy hand, nails pointed and varnished in black.

"Why hello, Amelia. I've heard all about you." She's had work. Botox or facelift or both.

"Lovely to meet you, Gwen," I say. "And congratulations to you both."

A sultry smile plays across Gwen's face as she drapes her arm around Beth. "Yes, my lovely little lone wolf here was quite the catch. Weren't you, my love?" She plants a kiss on Beth's blushing cheek, then rubs off the scarlet lipstick she's left behind.

"Gorgeous view," I say, turning to the vista. And it is. The sweeping views out across the Hudson and the glittering cityscape in nighttime mode is truly spectacular.

Gwen waves a hand as if it's nothing. "Yes, we're very lucky. Now, let's get you a drink, Amelia. What'll you have?"

For a second, I'm stumped. "Oh, a tonic, with a splash of lime?"

Gwen frowns, then tuts. "Nonsense." She turns to Beth. "Darling, get the woman a proper drink. G&T—large on the G. After all, we are celebrating here."

I protest but Gwen waves that hand again. "No arguments, young lady."

Beth gives me a look. "You okay with that?"

I give in and throw her a smile.

"Sure," I say. "A G&T would be great."

As the night wears on, I end up in the corner near a table laden with canapés. I bend to study the labels. Melon, mozzarella and prosciutto on skewers. Balsamic Beef Crostini with Herbed Cheese and Arugula. Smoked Salmon on Mustard-Chive and Dill Butter Toasts. Herbed Biscuit Bites with Ricotta Cream and Onion Jam.

The waiter with a large bottle of champagne is circulating again and offers to refill my glass. Earlier, when Gwen insisted everyone toast to true love, I had switched from G&T to champagne. The toast came after Beth's and Gwen's teary-eyed speeches.

Gwen's declaration was, of course, delivered with finesse, peppered with humor and awash with sentiment. Dabbing at her tears ("Golly, I'm such a crybaby"), Gwen spoke about how she and Beth had first met in a coffee shop called Holy Cow in Greenwich Village ("Our eyes locked over a salmon and caper bagel"), then their first date at the Metropolitan Museum of Art ("It was hard to believe that Beth had even seen the inside of any museum let alone the MET"), and Gwen's proposal, a very grand affair involving a helicopter, romantic roof top dinner, and mariachi band.

By comparison, Beth's speech was short and read from a handwritten note. Her nerves were so bad that her voice shook more than the paper in her hand. But there was no doubting the heartfelt nature of her speech, in which she spoke of her undying true love and admiration for Gwen, the soulmate she never thought she would ever find. There was not a dry eye left in the house.

That was an hour ago, and a fair few glasses of champagne had been consumed by partygoers since then, including me. Any plans I had about leaving early had long since dissolved. I was actually having a good time. It was impossible not to with everyone in such a positive and celebratory mood. Plus, I had no reason to rush home to an empty apartment, and no work commitments the next morning to consider. In actual fact, I had no commitments to consider at all. And here, inside the lush surroundings of Gwen and Beth's love nest, I was safe. I was also released, albeit temporarily, from the burden of having to keep alert for any malevolent forces out to get me.

So it is an easy yes to more champagne, and the waiter is only too happy to oblige, refilling my gold-rimmed flute to the brim.

"So what do you think?" says the woman to my left. She has a Cruella de Vil haircut and piercing blue eyes. "Degas or Cézanne?"

"Sorry?" I say.

A small group of six are huddled around a little bronze sculpture on a pedestal. It's of a lithe young girl, a ballet dancer, her elegant neck stretched to the heavens, slender back leg gracefully extended behind her.

"The sculpture. Do you think it's a Degas or a Cézanne?"

Everyone looks at me expectantly. A few eyes lower to my cane.

"Oh, I'm not much good with art," I say, a little brazenly. Am I slurring my speech?

Cruella looks miffed, then turns back to the sculpture. "Definitely a Degas."

Another woman nods, younger than Cruella de Vil, with cleavage that looks store-bought. "I agree. The little strumpet has Degas written all over her."

A guy, a trendy thirty-something dressed in a silver double-breasted paisley waistcoat, holding a bottle of champagne in one hand and a glass in the other, bends down to peer at the tiny statue. "I didn't even know Degas did sculpture."

"Oh, Dan, you luddite," laughs Cruella, smacking him on the arm.

"That's abuse!" he says, faking outrage.

He fills his glass, then everyone else's, including mine. I sip and it feels good to be part of something, simply having fun at a party. The woman with the store-bought cleavage shakes my hand and tells me her name is Denise.

"Amelia," I say.

"So how do you know Gwen? Were you in the academy with her?"

I shake my head. "I'm a friend of Beth's."

"Beth's a trouper," says Dan, taking a swill of champagne. "I can't imagine Gwen's easy to live with."

"Oh, Dan. You Judas. I dare you to say that to her face," says Cruella.

"Well, I think they make a very cute couple, don't you agree, Amelia?" says Denise.

I nod. "They look very happy together."

"I give it a year, eighteen months tops," says Dan. He gets another slap on the arm for that one.

But everyone laughs at his audacity. I find myself laughing, too. I go with it, seeing myself from above, forgetting the bad times, just being normal, zero pain in my half foot. I feel like my old self.

"Wait a minute." It's from the woman with the red Chanel frames, late twenties, no makeup. She's been silent this whole time. "Don't I know you from somewhere?"

"I don't think so," I say.

She stares at me and looks at my cane. She rubs her thumb along her lower lip, thinking. Her face clears as the light goes on in her head and I know what's coming. I feel utterly nauseous.

"You're that girl. The wilderness chick."

And just like that all eyes jump on me, half-appalled, half-pitying.

I could lie. I could say that it wasn't me. I could say that this happens sometimes, that I am mistaken for that poor wretch, because apparently, ha-ha, I look a lot like her. A doppelganger. Some people are spitting images of Sandra Bullock or Miley Cyrus, but my misfortune is to look like that wilderness chick who was kidnapped, raped, and left for dead in the Oregon wilderness. But I don't lie; instead I say—

"Well, you got me there." I aim for funny but come across as strange and slightly demented.

"Oh, I remember reading about that," one of them says. I don't know who because I am looking everywhere except their faces.

"That must have been rough."

"What was it like being out there the woods with that lunatic?" says Dan.

They wait for me to say something but I don't.

Dan wrinkles his nose. "Still a bit raw?"

"Maybe she doesn't want to talk about it, Dan," says Denise.

Dan ignores her and continues, "I know they say you faked it, but the thing with the foot, I always said, no way you can't make that shit up."

"Jesus, Dan, that's real classy."

But Dan's on a roll. "Did they ever catch him? The oil refinery dude."

"Rex Hawkins," Red Chanel Glasses pipes in.

"Yeah, that guy," says Dan.

I swallow. "No."

"You're joking! You mean he's still out there? Oh, man, that would freak me out," says Dan, shaking his head.

"Dan," this time hissed through Denise's perfect set of veneers. "You're scaring the poor thing."

I put down my champagne glass. "If you'll excuse me."

I don't wait for goodbyes. Behind me there are hushed reprimands for Dan. I don't even try to find Beth. I just leave.

19

The cold air blasts me when I exit the building. I'm unsteady on my feet. I've had way too much to drink. My muscles feel weak, my brain foggy. I'm teary too. I think of the way they looked at me back there, with their pity and blatant curiosity. All they really wanted were the grubby details. That's all anybody really wants. I've become a form of entertainment. A real-life, walking-talking episode of *Dateline*. I try to recall a time when I wasn't different, when I was just part of the crowd and not the object of such unwelcome attention. Will I ever get back to just being me? Just plain, old ordinary Amelia Kellaway?

I stop and blink heavily at the street sign. Carter Avenue. I have gone the wrong way. I look around. It's dark and isolated and I'm drunk. Focus, God damn it, you're getting yourself into a mess.

I turn back and try to locate Beth's apartment but only get more confused in the warren of laneways.

I start to panic. My limbs are lazy with alcohol and I will never be able to defend myself.

I look around for a cab. I don't usually take cabs because it means getting into cars with men I don't know, but tonight I'm willing to make an exception. I just want to get home. But there's not a cab in sight, even if I wanted one.

It begins to rain and I keep walking. More of a staggering trudge than a walk because a strange type of numbness has inhabited every part of my body and given me leaden limbs. Then I remember it's not just the alcohol that's affecting me, it's the tramadol mixed with the alcohol. I berate myself for being so careless.

I go deeper into the neighborhood. Eyes watch from apartments. Dark doorways threaten to pounce.

I lose my sense of direction and have to double back. I am getting so lost. I stop and look around, dumbfounded. The concrete jungle of Tribeca is turning green. I can smell moss, the earth, my own fear, the sticks and stones under my feet. The pine. I rest my hand on the side of the building and suck in air. The haunting sound of creaking pines. The whoosh above my head. The dart of a sparrow. The cry of a wolf. Him behind me, chasing. Sweating now, I can't breathe.

Someone touches my shoulder. "You okay?"

With a jolt I'm brought back to reality. It's a woman from the party.

"You don't look so good."

"Which way to the subway?"

"Two blocks, turn right."

I hurry away.

She shouts behind me, "Hey, why don't you let me call you a cab!"

But I keep going, until, mercifully, the subway sign appears up ahead.

20

Somehow, I make it to my usual spot in the park across from my apartment. I stand staring at the building. My vision is blurred and it's hard to focus. I force myself to count the floors slowly. First. Second. Third. Fourth. Fifth. Sixth. Seventh. Eighth. I scan each balcony, then study my own.

I repeat the process, beginning with the ground floor again, then up to fourth, my floor. I stop. Something's wrong. The blind in the living room is different. One side of the slats are all the way down. The other side is open a crack like I left it. I try to think back to when I departed for Beth's. Did I miss that side of the blinds? But I'm sure I performed the checking sequence three times. Or was that the time before? I try my very best to remember but my brain refuses to work.

The lights go off in my apartment. Oh God. That's bad. Then I tell myself, settle. It's okay. Just the timer doing its job. But now, with the lights out inside the apartment, I can't see a damn thing and I'm unable to check for any human-sized shadows or any movement back and forth.

I think of something. I dig inside my bag for my wallet and phone. I find the business card and punch in the number.

Ethan North's voice fills the line.

"Have you been in my apartment?" I say.

"Amelia?"

"Just answer me. Have you been here?"

"No, I haven't been anywhere near your place. What's going on? Are you okay? You sound upset."

I start to cry. I can't contain it. "Someone's in there."

"What?"

"Please…I can't." I choke on the words. "He's in there."

"Who's in there?"

"Him…Rex…Oh God, I'm going to be sick."

"Where are you?"

"At the park across the street."

"Stay there. I'm on my way."

21

Less than twenty minutes later, I hear Ethan calling my name. I'm in the bushes, hiding. He calls my name again. I stand up. He sees me, and I catch the shocked look on his face. I want to crawl into a hole and never come out.

"Jesus, Amelia," he says when he reaches me. "You're shaking like a leaf. What happened?"

I can't speak. I'm gulping air, sobbing like a frightened little girl.

"Take a deep breath."

I try. It hurts.

"It's okay. We'll stay here as long as you need."

I feel him beside me, his warmth, his goodness. I begin to calm down.

"Can we please sit," I splutter.

"Sure."

He escorts me to the bench near the climbing bars and we sit.

"Better?" he says.

I nod.

"You've been drinking," he says. A matter of fact, no judgment. I'm ashamed anyway. It means he can smell it on me.

"Drugs too?" he says.

I shake my head no, then catch myself. "Prescription. Tramadol for my foot."

He glances at my building. "You come here to check your apartment?"

"Yes."

"You're that afraid of him coming back?"

I don't answer. God, what must he think of me?

"It's a disorder," I say, finally. "I'm getting help for it."

He looks up at the apartment, frowning. "And the blinds? They're not the same way you left them?"

"Every time I leave the apartment, I always make sure both blinds are lowered to the same height, with the slats slanted at a forty-five-degree angle. Every time. Without fail. I've never not done it."

He considers this for a moment.

"But it's possible, isn't it?" he says. "That you made a mistake this one time?"

I shake my head. "I don't agree."

But I'm already having doubts. I've been so distracted with the job suspension, the blackouts, the empty envelope, the lack of sleep.

"Did you have anything to drink before you went out?" he says.

"No."

He gets to his feet. "I guess there's only one way to find out."

I pull on his arm. "Wait. It's not safe to go in there. Rex Hawkins is a very dangerous man."

Ethan shows me his Glock the waistband of his pants. "I'm not past a bit of danger myself."

He takes me to his car, a beat-up, aqua-colored Honda, and guides me into the passenger's seat.

"Lock the doors," he says through the window.

Then he turns and heads inside my building. I wait nervously. The clock on the dash is one hour too slow. 2:13 a.m. God, poor Ethan, I can't believe I dragged him out of bed for this.

I watch the clock. 2:20. 2:25. 2:30. Why is he taking so long? I tell myself to relax. He's just being careful like I told him. It's a good thing. 2:35. 2:40. I look at the building door. My stomach churns. He's taking forever. 2:45. This isn't right. It's been way too long. The door to my building opens and I hold my breath. But it's just Mr. Leibowitz, the Polish man from the second floor, taking his dachshund, Cindy, for a bathroom break.

Where the hell is Ethan? I try calling his cell. No answer.

Mr. Leibowitz passes by me after Cindy does her business. He gives me a look, but doesn't say anything. He reaches our building and pauses on the steps, half-turning to eyeball the Honda as if he's deciding whether to come over or not.

The door opens behind him. It's Ethan. I've never felt such relief.

Mr. Leibowitz disappears inside and Ethan half-jogs to the Honda.

"All clear," he says.

"You sure? You looked everywhere?"

He pauses. "I think you made a mistake."

I burst into tears. "I'm sorry."

He touches my shoulder. "Hey, it's okay. Let's get you inside."

"Will you stay with me tonight?"

He looks shocked.

"I'm not sure it would be such a good idea," he says.

I feel like a complete idiot. I nod. "No, you're right, God, I'm sorry. It's too much to ask. You've done so much already." I bite my lip, "It's just that…well…I'm scared."

He falls silent. He glances over his shoulder and looks at my apartment, then turns back to me.

He picks up my purse. "I'll take the couch."

22

I stir in the wee small hours. I've been dreaming about my dead father. I reach for the sound of his voice but can't get it back. There's a painful squeeze beneath my rib cage I haven't felt for years. Groggy, I lift my head to look at the clock. 5:47 a.m. Last night returns in a flood. The party. The panic attack. Ethan North.

I sit up. My head spins and I nearly vomit into my hand. I grab a fistful of blankets and sway there, on the edge of the abyss, praying for it to pass. Eventually it does, or at least enough so I can push aside my bed covers and get to my feet without falling over. My mouth feels like sandpaper. I need water.

Edging slowly out of my bedroom, I stop dead in my tracks when I see the door to the spare room wide open. Ethan North is kneeling on the floor poring over my precious files.

"What are you doing?"

His head jerks up. "Amelia."

"Get out!"

Ethan scrambles to his feet. "I was looking for the switchboard. The lights came on when I was sleeping on the couch."

My legs shake in anger. "Bullshit. You were snooping."

"No, Amelia, I wasn't," he says.

"I know you're lying because I always keep this door locked. The key is in a box next to my bed."

Ethan looks at me. "I don't know what to say. It wasn't locked."

"That's impossible."

But even as I say it, I begin to doubt myself. Could it be another slip?

Ethan turns to look at the wall. "Why didn't you tell me?"

It's all there for him to see. Photographs of the three murdered women. Photographs of the seventeen missing women. Shots of Rex Hawkins's ranch and oil refinery compound, from when it was active, to its current abandoned state. The possible identikit images of what he may look like now, with or without hair, gray or black or blond, with mustache or full beard or goatee or sideburns, glasses or contacts. And all my Post-it note scribblings, recording observations, possible connections, questions, further avenues of inquiry.

Ethan looks astounded. "All this work. It must have taken you forever."

I limp over and shove him toward the door.

"Get out!"

"Don't be upset, Amelia. I just want to help."

I shove harder. "I don't want your help. Get out of my home."

He doesn't budge. "You think he's done this before."

"Ethan, please," I say, close to tears. "I'm not comfortable with this."

He takes me by the shoulders. "Amelia, I'm not going anywhere until you tell me what's going on."

23

He makes us tea and brings it back to the spare room. I remain standing, the mug hot in my hand. It's disconcerting having him here in my space, the center of operations, the inner workings of my mind on display for him to see. He takes the seat at my desk.

"I'm listening," he says.

"No one else believes me. Why should you?"

"Try me."

I exhale. I wonder how much I should tell him, what I should leave out, what I should leave in. But Ethan's no dummy and it's all on the wall.

"All right," I say.

I turn around and tap the first photo. A blue-eyed woman with red hair and a wide smile.

"Shelly White, thirty-two. Shelly went missing after a day hike with her boyfriend along the Oregon-Washington border. Her boyfriend returned without her, and when she didn't show up after four hours, he notified police, told them he and Shelly had a spat about his ex-girlfriend and she stormed off. No one believed him, of course. They questioned him for over eight hours. He insisted it was all true. Finally, police decided to go look for Shelly but there was no sign of her. Ten days later a hunter finds her body in a shallow grave. Strangled and sustained sexual assault. The boyfriend was charged, went on trial, got acquitted. There was no evidence he had ever been involved at all."

I pause. My heart's going a million miles an hour. I look at Ethan to see if he's following.

"Go on," he says.

I point to the second photo. Another blue-eyed woman, although this one has cropped brown hair and is kissing a dog, a black Lab with a red bandana tied around its neck.

"Amanda Buckley, twenty-eight. Amanda liked to run the trails along the Oregon coast with her dog, Pip. Fit and athletic, she ran at least every couple of weeks. One Sunday in November she went on a run with Pip. When she didn't return by sundown, her roommate put out an alert. Authorities conducted a three-day ground search within a fifty-mile radius and found no sign of the dog or Amanda. On the fourth day, a hiker saw Pip hanging from a tree, his mistress's sports bra tied around his neck. One week goes by, then two, three, a month. Then a truck driver on a bathroom stop spots something off road on the Oregon Coast Road. It was Amanda's body. Again, sexual assault, strangulation, shallow grave."

"But how could forensics tell after all that time?"

I raise my hand to silence him. "I'll get to that."

I unpin the third photo. Young, beautiful, deep green eyes and wavy blonde hair.

"Olivia Wendell, nineteen, left California bound for a solo hike along the Oregon coast. She hitched most of the way. Truck drivers mostly, and a couple of families on their way north. According to Willis Smart, a seventy-year-old grandpa from Seattle, he dropped Olivia here." I point to the photograph of the gas station pinned to the map. "The last person to see her was a clerk who sold her Little Debbie snack cakes."

I glance at the photograph and swallow. I smell pine and gasoline.

Ethan stares at me. "Is that the place where he grabbed you?"

He's done his homework.

"Yeah."

"You want to take a break?"

I shake my head and drink some tea. I look at the photo of Olivia again.

"Six weeks later they found Olivia's body in a shallow, snow-covered grave, raped and strangled. Some snowmobilers ran right over her, sliced the top of her skull."

Ethan winces. "Jesus."

"Yeah, the autopsy photos are brutal."

He pauses. "And you think it's him?"

I turn away. "You don't believe me."

"I didn't say that."

"They were kept alive," I look at him, "like me, for long periods, and taken from the same geographical location I was. Two women before me, one after, that I know of."

"What about those ones?" he says, nodding to the corkboard and the seventeen photographs of other women.

"Missing. All around the same area. Within the last five to ten years. Similar physical appearance."

"A serial killer?"

I catch it, the unmistakable look of pity, and I'm suddenly angry. "I'm not trying to convince you of anything, Ethan. You're the one who asked me to walk you through this."

"Amelia, you know how easy it is to make everything fit. You're a lawyer. You do it for a living." He gestures to the wall. "That's not evidence. It's coincidence at best. I'm not sure I see a pattern here. Yes, these women were raped and strangled, but that's not exactly unusual."

I cross my arms. "I didn't expect you to understand."

"Isn't this just you holding on, unable to let go? Isn't this part of your disorder?"

"You think I'm crazy?"

"I'm not saying that. In your position I would probably be drawing the same conclusions. But that doesn't mean those conclusions are correct. Amelia, don't you see? You aren't a neutral party here. There's no way you can analyze the evidence impartially. It would be impossible for anyone in your position to do that."

I refuse to look at him. "I'd like you to leave."

"Oh, Amelia, come on."

"I'm serious, Ethan. Go now."

He stands. "If that's what you want."

"It is."

He takes the mug of cold tea from my hands. "I'll see myself out then."

I know I should thank him for helping me last night but I turn my back and crouch to pick up the files.

"I could run some names if you like," he says, hovering at the door. "I've got a buddy who works national missing persons cases."

"Don't do me any favors."

"Are you always this belligerent?"

I return the files to the desk and turn to face him.

"I believe I asked you to leave."

He stares at me. "You should be rebuilding your life, putting the horror of what happened behind you."

"You don't know what you're talking about."

"All this," he says gesturing to the photos, "it's heartbreaking, Amelia. You're not doing yourself any favors."

"I don't need your pity."

"That's not what I meant."

"Isn't it?"

He lets out a breath. "All right. Okay. I'm leaving." He slips by me and then looks over his shoulder. "You know where to find me."

24

It takes days for my anger to subside. I feel like I've exposed my soul to the world. How dare Ethan pry. How dare he judge. How dare he pick my thinking apart. I never asked for his opinion.

He's been around for three days straight to check up on me. But I've ignored his knocking, just like I've ignored his phone calls. I don't want to talk to him. It's childish I know, but part of me wants to punish him.

Beth has called, too. To see why I've missed our sessions at the gym. But I can't face anyone right now. I can't stand their doubt, the look of pity on their faces, at me, in my sorry mental state.

I study the wall over and over, trying to see what Ethan sees. Where he sees a bunch of unrelated crimes, I see a pattern. But could he be right? Is it simply all speculation? What he said about lawyers making up stories is true. It *is* my job to create workable theories of the case, to make assumptions to fill in gaps, and sometimes those assumptions are wrong.

I think of John Liber and how many months it took me to work up the courage to share what I'd found with him. But as soon as the words were out of my mouth, I knew I had made a mistake. Doubt had clouded his face in an instant. Then he said, *Kiddo, you're chasing shadows here*, and urged me to see Lorna. The implication was clear. He thought I was delusional, and for a while there I thought maybe he was right.

At that point, I considered burying the whole thing. Then I discovered Olivia Wendell, so I went to the FBI instead. I showed them all the data I collated, systematically walked them through the times, dates, locations, similar fact pattern evidence. And unlike John Liber, they seemed interested and promised to make further inquiries. Only they didn't. What they did was stop returning my calls. And now this latest defeat with Ethan...

Olivia, Amanda, and Shelly stare out at me from the wall. Happy in their respective elements. Completely unaware of the tragedy about to befall them. Sheltered, just as I had been. Only I wasn't like them because I survived.

And the missing women, seventeen now, but growing. These women didn't simply disappear into a black hole. No, they fit his type, his preferred locations, his MO. It is chilling.

It's him, I know it is. These murders and disappearances have his hands all over them. I just need that elusive strand of evidence to tie it all together.

I study the photograph of Olivia. The cause for most concern because she came eighteen months after the incident with me. It proved he was still at it. How many more Olivias are out there? How many more Olivias could be prevented if he was caught?

My half foot burns. I need to bathe it in saline and reapply the antiseptic cream. But I reach for my laptop instead. The foot can wait. I open up my web browser and start searching again.

25

At 4 a.m. I wake up in the middle of the spare room floor with someone standing over me. I scream and scramble backward. But when I look again, I see that no one is there. I take a moment to get my bearings. My laptop is open, a satellite image of the Oregon coast on the screen. It comes back to me. I'd spent most of the night on the net trawling for leads and more possible victims. But hours of searching newspaper archives, court records, missing person forums came up empty.

Doubt seeps in. Maybe Ethan is right. Maybe everything is a figment of my imagination. Maybe I'm descending deeper into some delusional state.

It could be a repeat of the tulips and pine cones. Everyone thought I was sending them to myself. Oh, they never said anything overtly but the suggestion was always there. The police. My mother. John Liber. I remember raising it with Lorna during a session. She had sat there impassively so I couldn't be sure what her view was.

"What do you think about that?" she had said.

"What do I think? I think it's ridiculous. Why the hell would I send things to myself? Besides, I would know if I'd done something like that. I would remember." I looked at her then. "Wouldn't I?"

She'd shrugged. "Not necessarily. It could be some form of stress-induced automatism."

"Do you think I did it, Lorna?"

I had expected to get the usual noncommittal stance from her but instead she said—

"To tell you the truth, Amelia, I simply don't know."

I limp to the bathroom and examine my foot. It's a mess. I spend the next hour cleaning it, gingerly bathing it in warm saline solution, extracting the gunk a little at a time, applying copious amounts of antiseptic cream. I bind it tightly in a clean bandage to prevent the swelling from getting worse.

Then I go to bed to see if I can get some sleep before daybreak.

26

I'm asleep when a persistent knock on the front door wakes me. I try to ignore it. But whoever it is, they're not giving up. Then a text. From Ethan.

Please come to the door. I need to make sure you're OK. I roll onto my back and stare at the ceiling. God. Sighing deeply, I drag myself from my nest of blankets and trudge through the apartment to the front door.

"Go away, Ethan." My voice is hoarse because I haven't spoken in days.

"I'm not leaving until you open up."

"I'm sorry you wasted a trip."

"You're being stubborn."

I soften a little. My mother used to call me stubborn when I was a little kid.

"Please, Amelia."

I give in and open the door. He stares at me, stunned. I must look rough but I'm too drained to care.

He holds up a bag. "I brought oranges."

I'm touched. "You didn't need to do that."

"I wanted to." He slips past me and places the fruit on the counter. "There's a good farmer's market in Park Slope. I sometimes go there on the weekend to get my pop some fresh fruit and vegetables. Makes a change from all the microwave slop they feed him in the home." Ethan glances around my gloomy apartment, chin nods toward the lowered blinds. "It's a sunny day out there, you know."

"Is it?" I say, dropping to the sofa.

He frowns. "Your limp is worse than before. Is your foot sore? Need me to drive you to a doctor?"

"I'm not an invalid."

He plunges his hands in his pockets. "Of course you're not. Sorry." He pauses, looking awkward. "Actually, Amelia, I was hoping we could talk about something."

"Oh?"

"Rex Hawkins."

I shudder. Even the name makes me want to be sick.

"I think you know what I'm going to say," continues Ethan.

I turn away.

"Amelia?" he presses.

"I don't know what you think you've found out but I'm sure it isn't accurate."

He takes the seat opposite, rests his forearms on his knees, knits his hands together.

"After you walked me through your theory, I made some inquiries and spoke to the FBI." He watches me carefully. "They found Rex Hawkins's body two and a half years ago. But you know that already, don't you?"

There it is again. Doubt. Pity. Kindness. All rolled into one sweet package.

I shrug. "Even the FBI makes mistakes."

It sounds hollow and I wish I could do better.

He shakes his head in disbelief. "You can't honestly believe that. There's DNA. It's incontrovertible. Rex Hawkins is dead."

I lean back. "He isn't dead."

Ethan raises his eyebrows. "He's never been seen or heard from since. The women you've identified in your war room are someone else's victims, not his."

I shake my head. "I would know if he was dead. I would feel it."

"But, Amelia, don't you see?" his tone softening. "There's no need for you to worry about him anymore. All this crazy checking is completely unnecessary. You can let it go now. Get on with your life. You're a free woman."

"Crazy?"

"I didn't mean it like that."

I'm so angry, I can barely speak. "Don't interfere."

He holds his hands up and stands. "I know, I know. Get out. Leave. I don't need help from anyone. Especially you, Ethan."

We stare at each other for a moment.

"You deserve better than this."

His voice is soft, like the click of the door behind him.

When Ethan's gone, I sit in the quiet. Thinking and not thinking. I think of Thanksgiving the previous year when my family gathered at Mom's for Thanksgiving dinner in upstate New York. My mother needed a bowl for the green beans and had asked me to retrieve Nana May's antique Asprey crystal bowl from the cedar chest in her bedroom. That's when I found the scrapbook with the newspaper clippings. Precisely cut and meticulously glued down on blotting paper, my sorry saga recorded for prosperity. From the first report of my rescue, to a catalog of my injuries, to a telescopic shot of me leaving the hospital in a wheelchair.

As I sat on my mother's bed leafing through the scrapbook, I realized how sheltered I had been. I had never seen the reports about myself. Those first few weeks after my return were a blur of surgeries and therapy. The protective circle of people who cared for me had sheltered me from the publicity and allowed me to recover.

As I looked through the scrapbook, it became clear that my miserable story had been hijacked. Rather than a story of survival, it become an archaic warning tale about what can go wrong when a woman strays too far from home. That made me sick. The last thing I wanted was to discourage young women from embarking on adventure and experiencing personal growth.

When I got to the final page, I saw a clipping about Matthew, my first love, the man I thought I would marry. Some reporter had tried to bait him into commenting on my condition as he left the hospital. There was a shot of him, in mirrored aviators, sliding into his Valencia Orange BMW Roadster. The photo reawakened a painful memory of Matthew's visit to the hospital and his inability to look me in the eye. I know he felt responsible. He was supposed to come with me on the trek but backed out at the last minute.

I never saw him again after the hospital visit. He moved to California to work for a commercial firm there, married then divorced a year later. Not that I blame him for leaving me. Who would want a cripple with an ugly half foot and a hearty dose of PTSD?

I'm not sure why my mother saved the clippings. I never asked. I simply returned the scrapbook to its place and retrieved Nana May's pretty Asprey crystal bowl and we ate our green beans, along with the rest of dinner.

I get to my feet and nearly fall down. A searing pain grips my useless, mutilated foot. Wow. It's so bad I clutch the edge of the sofa to catch my breath. I inhale and exhale. Three times. Then once more.

I shuffle to the counter, rifle through my purse for some tramadol, and take two with a glass of water. Within thirty minutes, my foot feels a whole lot better, good enough to be able to hobble to the spare room.

I stare at the faces of the murdered and missing women, my Post-it notes, the identikit images. All the years of work. All the thinking, the putting together, the scenarios I have built up in my mind. I stare at the photo of Rex Hawkins. I go in close. Those friendly blue eyes. The lips that formed such easy lies. The hands that nearly choked the life out of me. I can almost smell the Tide on his freshly laundered shirt.

Ethan is right. This isn't real evidence. My thinking has become distorted. I am distorted. Rex Hawkins is dead.

Snatching fistfuls from the wall, I tear it all down, every last bit, until everything is just garbage under my feet. Breathing hard, I stand looking at the empty wall. Then I put my head in my hands and cry.

*

I don't leave my bed for four days. I exist in a semi-conscious state. Walking a tightrope between wakefulness and sleep. Gambling with heavy doses of tramadol to quiet the pain in my foot.

Nightmares stalk me. I am lost in the forest, surrounded by wolves. There is the dreadful weight of dirt on my chest. He is chasing me, gaining fast, shouting my name.

When sleep refuses to come, I lie on my back and stare into darkness. Thoughts pass through me like a dirty wind. Sounds, too, seep through the timber and plaster. Fragments of everyday life. Murmurs. Voices raised in a fight. The groan of pipes. The smell of cooking food.

All the while, I lie here, the involuntary eavesdropper, lost in a black hole of time. The better part of myself urges me to get up, call Lorna, my mother, anyone. Let some light in. Move. But the misery is stronger. It tells me I might be better off dead.

On the fourth day the tramadol runs out. The pain in my foot is unbearable. I'm sure it's infected. Heat is rising up my ankle and I have to get medicine. There's no avoiding it.

I leave the cradle of my bed and hunt the apartment for a prescription from the doctor I saved some time ago. I find it buried in a drawer beneath a pile of utility bills.

I glance down at the clothes I haven't changed in days. I should shower and put on some fresh ones, look less like a dope fiend. Instead, I finger-comb my hair, pull on a coat, and leave.

Thankfully, the drug store is only at the end of my street. Even so, it's hard going. I take it slow, biting back pain, my scrawny, white-knuckled hand strangling my trembling cane.

By the time I step inside the drug store, I'm sweating profusely. I pause next to a display of Johnson's baby powder and toilet paper to catch my breath. The dank box of a store is cramped and disorganized, with products displayed haphazardly next to each another. Diapers and window cleaner. Cosmetics and trash bags. Prepaid mobile cards and soy-flavored rice cakes. Fluorescent strip-lighting and water-stained ceiling panels only add to the gloom.

The pharmacy is located at the back of the store so I maneuver my way through narrow rows cluttered with all manner of items. Food. Sunglasses. Toothbrushes. Preschooler toys.

I pass by a construction worker studying the ingredients list on a tube of Bengay, humming to a Tears for Fears song playing through the scratchy store speakers.

I dig in my pocket for the prescription and place it on the counter.

"Can you fill this, please."

The pharmacist is a mid-thirties Korean-American man. Andy Cho, according to the name badge. A bit of a trendsetter by the looks of his over-styled hair and the checked salmon-pink shirt under his white pharmacist coat.

"It'll be ready in ten minutes or so, ma'am," says the smiling Andy Cho.

Ten minutes? I can't wait that long. I need pain relief now. I consider telling him it's urgent but decide that'll make him think I'm some sort of junkie, so I wait patiently by a carousel display of insoles and corn pads. Fitting, I think, given the current state of my foot. I wipe my face with the cuff of my coat. God, I'm so hot. And thirsty. I should go get a bottle of water but I don't have the energy.

A woman in a blue parka perusing a display of batteries one aisle over keeps checking me out. No doubt I look as bad as I feel. I pick up a magazine, bury my face in it, try to focus on an article about the latest advance in biomechanics. My vision blurs. I glance at the counter. I'm not sure how much longer I can hang on. Everything hurts. I bite my cheek to stop myself from yelling out.

Andy Cho reappears, frowning.

"I'm afraid there's a problem, ma'am."

"Oh?"

"Your prescription has expired."

"What? That can't be right."

He shows me the date on the prescription. It expired six months ago.

"I'm sorry. I can't fill it."

"But you could make an exception," I say. "Just this one time."

He pauses and looks at me. "Do you have an issue with narcotics, ma'am?"

My legs wobble. "What? No. It's my foot. Please, can you just fill the prescription? I think I might have an infection." I lick away beads of sweat on my upper lip.

"If you have an infection you should see a doctor."

"I don't need to see a doctor. The expired date is just a technicality, surely you can make an exception this one time."

Andy Cho folds the prescription in half and slides it across the counter. "I'd lose my license."

"I just need medicine for my foot…accident…the woods," I say, tripping over my words.

Andy Cho frowns. "The woods?"

"The woods, yeah." My tongue feels thick. Andy Cho is fading in and out. "Oh, the pain."

I reach for the carousel rack of insoles and go down.

28

Voices come to me in snatches. You're safe now. How much have you taken? Can you feel this? What's your name? Do you know what year it is? Hold still while we put on the brace.

I don't know where I am but I'm moving, being moved, slipping in and out of consciousness. An ambulance. I'm in the back of an ambulance. The woman putting a needle in my arm has the bluest eyes. Pretty cornflower blue. I want to tell her she has the bluest eyes I have ever seen but when I try to speak I can't. My tongue is dead in my mouth.

"Ba...." I say and slip away again.

When I come to, I try to sit up but my head is jammed between two polystyrene blocks. I feel the tape sticking to my forehead. A gentle hand on my shoulder pushes me down.

"Relax. You had a bad knock. We need to check your neck."

Oh my God, I have broken my neck. And I thought having a half foot was bad enough. I roll my eyes to the left. I'm in a world full of people. A nurse is taking someone's blood. A young boy has his arm in a splint. A man in a red beanie is fighting with a security guard. A busy ER department. Next to me a uniformed police officer is taking notes.

"And who is Rex Hawkins?" he says.

"What?"

"Is he your husband?"

I try to shake my head but can't because of the neck brace. I start crying.

"Calm down, ma'am."

I choke on my tears. I try to sit up. Hands press me back down. My heart races.

"No, don't! Please!" I yell.

A needle is quickly slipped into my arm and I fade out again.

When I wake, I'm still in the ER department but the police officer is gone and I'm free of the neck brace. I sit up and my stomach flips. A passing nurse shoves a container under my mouth just in time.

"Whoa there," she says.

I throw up good and proper.

"That's right, get it all out."

When I'm done, she gives me some water. I look at the IV drip going into my arm.

"Antibiotics," says the nurse. "Pretty savage infection by all accounts."

Oh god, they've amputated my leg. Panicked, I throw aside my bedsheet. Relief washes over me when I see that my leg is still intact, my foot in clean bandages.

"I want to go home."

"They're keeping you overnight for observation."

"No way. I have to get home."

She purses her lips. "You got a husband? Better half of some sort?"

I think of Ethan North.

"Yes," I say and reach for my phone.

29

Ethan and I sit in the living room in the failing light sipping the tea he has made. My eyes drop to the gold shield of his detective's badge clipped to his waistband, his holstered gun beneath his suit jacket.

"You were working," I say.

"I should never have left you," he says, almost bitterly.

He looks calmer now than he did before, when he had rushed into the hospital with sheer panic written all over his face, going from bed to bed trying to find me.

I look down at my tea. "You were right."

"I was?"

"About the links. There are none. It's all just speculation. Rex Hawkins is dead. There would've been some sign of him if he was alive." I look up. "I had an 'off-the-books' information analyst trying to track him down but she couldn't find any sign of him. And there's also the DNA evidence, of course. That's pretty irrefutable, isn't it? For some reason I just couldn't accept he was dead. I know how crazy that must sound."

Ethan raises an eyebrow. "Information analyst?"

"Yeah." I stare into my milky tea. "I never used to be like this, Ethan. I was happy once, confident, not this pathetic, broken person."

He reaches out and squeezes my hand. "You're not broken, Amelia. Sure, you're a different person than you were back then, you can't go through an experience like that and not be changed, but you'll forge a new path."

I start to cry. "I'm sorry. I'm tired."

"Hey." He puts down his mug and pulls me into a hug. "There's nothing to be sorry for."

He feels good and warm.

"Will you stay tonight?" I murmur into his shoulder.

He kisses the top of my head, rests his chin there, thinking.

"The sofa?" he says, finally.

"Not the sofa," I say.

*

I wake around 3 a.m. with Ethan lying next to me, fully clothed, on top of the covers. I watch his profile in the moonlight, that lip, hear the quiet warmth of his breath. He stirs and rolls on his side, blinks sleepily at me.

"Hey," he whispers.

I touch his cheek and feel stubble beneath my fingertips. "A true gentleman."

"Pop taught me well."

"Thank you for being here," I say.

He pauses. "You've been through a lot. I can only imagine."

I don't reply.

"I'm sorry," he says. "It's none of my business."

"No, it's okay." I swallow hard, take a breath. "For a long time, I was angry at myself, for being so naive."

"But you couldn't know what was going to happen. Hawkins manipulated you, took advantage of your good nature."

"Yes, I understand that now. He was so normal and nice, charming even. A cowboy type who certainly didn't appear like an abductor in waiting. When he asked me to help him with that spare tire, I never suspected a thing. I couldn't believe what was happening when he pushed me into the trunk of the car and took me to the woods. It was just so surreal, like I was trapped inside some kind of bizarre B-movie."

I lapse into silence. Ethan remains quiet beside me.

"I was raped, but you know that already. Everybody knows that," I say.

He gives me a squeeze. "I read about it in the papers."

I laugh sourly. "He even apologized for doing it." I shake my head in disbelief. "He was definitely big on playing mind games. He even said he would let me go then changed his mind."

"That's cruel."

"Yes."

"I read that you tried to get away."

I nod. "Twice. Each time he caught me. That last time he strangled me and dumped me in a dirt grave."

I shudder at the memory of his hands around my throat. "I managed to dig my way out, spent weeks lost in the wilderness, et cetera, et cetera...I'm sure you know the rest."

"It's an incredible story, Amelia. Something like that would have done most people in."

"Luck."

"No way. Luck had nothing to do with it. It was all down to you. You have a source of inner strength that you're not even aware of." He kisses my cheek. "You're an inspiration."

I feel myself blush. "So that's my sad story."

He pulls me into an embrace. "Thank you for trusting me enough to tell me."

"You want to join me in here where it's warm?"

I feel him study me in the darkness. "You think that's a good idea?"

"I think it's the best idea I've had in ages."

30

He calls in a few favors and takes the weekend off. We spend it together in a bubble. Outside, rain blisters the windows. Sleet too. Reminders that New York will soon be in the lead up to Christmas. With dark nights and snowfall. And all the transportation chaos that those things bring with them. But for now, all that seems far off, and I'm content to stay indoors with Ethan, furnace pounding out heat, dozing on the sofa while Ethan watches Netflix or baseball or motorsports on my laptop.

We feast on takeout—Thai, Indian, Mexican—which Ethan dutifully goes out to pick up every night, returning to the apartment clutching plastic bags and smelling of the city and shaking droplets from his coat. Then with our stomachs full, Ethan tells me more about his life, his long-departed mother who died when he was fifteen from kidney disease, his beloved Pop who lives in a geriatric care home, his decision to become a police detective and the impact that's had on his life, a divorce a decade back, a gastric ulcer, the unsolved cases that haunt him.

I lie there listening, taking in the timbre of his voice, his gentle presence in my space. I feel safe and at home. Slowly I begin to think that it could really be possible for me to forge a new path, one where the past doesn't dictate my future life.

All too soon, Monday morning arrives and Ethan has to go to work. He emerges from the bathroom, freshly showered and shaved, but in the same clothes he's been wearing for three days. I fight the urge to tell him not to go. Take the week off, I want to say, just stay here with me.

"You need me to come over tonight?" he says, shrugging into his coat.

"I'll be okay."

"You sure?"

I nod and see him to the door.

"Thank you," I say. "For this weekend."

He takes me by the shoulders and looks me in the eye.

"You need anything, you call. You're not alone in this, you understand, Amelia?"

I smile and give him a salute. "Understood, Detective North."

31

Lorna manages to squeeze me in at 2:20 p.m. It will be the first time I have been out of the apartment since the hospital. Without thinking, I begin the checking process. It's not until I am testing the window latch in my bedroom that I realize what I'm doing. I'm annoyed at myself. I've accepted that Rex Hawkins is dead so there is no need for this ridiculous behavior anymore.

I pause, take an internal audit on how I'm feeling. Tense? Panicked? Anxious? All the usual emotions that drive the checking process. I smile. I feel none of these things. I drop to the end of the bed. I feel good, actually, lighter. I think of Ethan. My heart does a little flip. The beginnings of love.

So, yes, there has been a change. Progress. The checking is a habit, an ingrained pattern, that needs to be undone. That's all. I can do this. I can forge a new path ahead.

So I permit myself one round of checking, and only one, and by the time I leave the apartment I already feel like I have won some sort of challenge.

*

Lorna looks worried when she greets me.

"Amelia, I've been concerned. I'm glad you reached out."

Her eyes run over my body, my face, my eyes, my wrists. I know she lost a patient a few months back. I overheard the receptionist talking about it. Bath. Hot water. Razor blades.

"Thanks for fitting me in."

I follow her into her office and we take our seats. She smooths down her lilac skirt and delivers her usual opening question.

"So, Amelia, where would you like to begin?"

I hesitate. I pour myself some water, take a sip, put my glass back down.

Finally, I look at her. "Lorna, I've been lying to you. For months. Years even."

She nods slowly. "Okay."

"And I don't want to do that anymore."

I tell her all of it. How bad the checking was. How diminished and lost I had become. My serial killer theory. Hiring Chris and my obsession to track Rex Hawkins down, even though logically I knew he was dead. Lorna listens intently. Tries to keep her face passive. But she has to be hurt and I feel bad. I know how much she cares and genuinely wants to help. She's a diligent therapist who demands very high standards of herself so my betrayal must be a low blow.

"Sorry," I say, finally.

She nods. "Thank you for being honest."

"I mean it, Lorna. You've been good to me. I told you I'd always be honest with you and I wasn't."

"This isn't about me and my feelings, Amelia. You should be proud of yourself. This is a significant breakthrough."

"There's something else."

"Go on."

"A man."

Lorna's a little taken aback. "A romantic relationship?"

"Yes, I think so."

"You think so?"

131

I feel myself blush. "He's nice. Too nice for me probably."

"You are a whole person, Amelia, worthy of love. Everyone has trauma at some point in their lives."

"Even you?"

She pauses and I think I'm going to get the usual we're-here-to-talk-about-you-not-me line.

Lorna nods instead. "Yes. Even me."

She lets that sit for a moment, then says, "Tell me about him. Your new man."

Ethan's face comes to me and I can't help but smile. "He's a police detective. Soft. In a good way. Caring."

"And he knows about the incident?"

"He does."

"And what about you? Does he know about the checking?"

"He knows everything."

Lorna seems impressed. "Well, that's a fine start."

"Yes."

She tilts her head. "But you're scared?"

I chew the inside of my cheek. "A bit."

"That's understandable, Amelia. Emotional connections with an intimate partner can raise feelings of intense vulnerability."

"Yes."

"But you shouldn't let that hold you back. It's a great opportunity for transformation."

"You think so?"

She smiles. "Absolutely."

"What about my compulsion to check? Will it stop?"

"Be patient with yourself. It's going to take time."

"Okay."

"Remember, Amelia, slow and steady wins the race."

32

I step outside Lorna's building into fresh air. I feel good, invigorated. Coming clean to Lorna has taken a massive weight off my shoulders and standing there in the late autumn sun, I experience an overwhelming sense of gratitude for the people who care about me. Lorna, John Liber, my mother, Ethan.

The thought of Ethan brings a smile to my lips, and acting on impulse, I take out my phone and punch in his number.

"I changed my mind," I say.

"Well, hello to you too," he says. "What exactly did you change your mind about?"

"Let's have dinner at my place tonight. I'll cook."

He laughs. "Wow. Beautiful, smart, and she cooks."

"Don't overdo it, Detective. How does six sound?"

"Six it is."

There's a Whole Foods Market a few blocks over, so I go there and peruse the aisles like I know what I'm doing. It's been years since I cooked for anyone, let alone someone I want to impress.

What to have? Steak? Pasta? Chicken? In the end, I opt for simple and fresh and choose two fat salmon fillets, a premade wasabi mayo, a packet of organic rocket salad, and a tub of honey crisp gelato to finish. I pause at the wine section but decide against it. I'm still on meds, and don't want a repeat of last time. Instead I select a large bottle of cold pressed juice, blood orange and pomegranate, and hope that Ethan will like it.

On the way to the checkout, I spy some spectacular white lilies. I grab a bunch and end up dripping water all over myself. The checkout operator, a woman in her mid-fifties, left hand wrapped in a thermo-skin RSI glove, passes me a paper towel.

"Pretty flowers," she says.

"They're for a special dinner."

The woman smiles. "What's the occasion?"

I pause, thinking. "New beginnings."

When I get home, there's a letter waiting for me from the Bar Association. The disciplinary hearing is scheduled for next week, Tuesday at 10 a.m. I lower myself into my chair. The real world is intruding and I'm not sure I like it.

Dear Ms. Kellaway

Following an Attorney Grievance Committee investigation into your alleged violation of The Lawyers Code of Professional conduct, namely:

- *DR 7-102 [1200.33] Representing a Client Within the Bounds of the Law.*
- *DR 7-103 [1200.34] Performing the Duty of Public Prosecutor or Other Government Lawyer.*

The Committee finds there is a case to answer and the alleged misconduct is sufficiently serious to warrant a due process hearing.

The possible outcomes are censure, suspension, or disbarment. It could mean the end of my career. I'm suddenly overcome with sadness. All I ever wanted was to be a lawyer and help people. After my initial shaky entry into the profession through corporate law, a soulless and brutal arena, I discovered public prosecution and found my life's purpose. It's where I belong. To have that taken away would be devastating.

On the other hand, maybe disbarment is exactly what I deserve. Maybe I'm not a fit and proper person to be doing such an important job. Whether I like it or not, I showed a terrible lack of judgment and violated one of the most sacred rules that went to the heart of the accused having a fair trial. It was a terrible, terrible mistake. It could be that the most honorable thing to do is resign and hand in my license.

But when I think of not being a prosecutor anymore my stomach clenches. Turning my back on the job I love is not what I want, and I have so much more to give. No, I need to fight for this. Throw everything I have at putting things right. I take out my notepad and pen and begin writing my submission.

When Ethan knocks on the front door precisely at six, I'm caught off guard. I've been so absorbed on working on my submission I've lost track of time. I glance around my messy apartment. I had wanted to tidy it before he arrived. Too late now. My stomach flutters. I quickly check my appearance in the mirror and tuck a stray lock of hair behind my ear. I can't believe I feel this silly, worse than a teenage girl. I open the door.

"Hey," he says, giving me a peck on the cheek.

He's as nervous as I am and we both laugh.

"Let's not be awkward," I say.

"Ditto, that," he says, stepping inside the apartment. "Smells good."

I laugh. "I haven't even started cooking yet."

"I was talking about you."

"Oh, the detective knows how to flatter a lady."

"That's not the only thing in my bag of tricks."

I turn and head for the kitchen. "There's fresh juice in the fridge. I was going to get wine but after last time..." I feel myself color.

"Juice sounds good to me," he says.

I kick myself for not getting him some beer. A six-pack of whatever. I make a mental note to find out what he likes so I can get it for next time.

"Hope you like salmon," I say, digging into the back of the cupboard for a frying pan.

"You bet. I could eat that stuff all day."

Ethan pours us each a juice and takes a seat at the counter. He glances at my notepad next to the empty fruit bowl.

"Looks official," he says, eyes running over my chicken scratches.

I place the salmon fillets in the sizzling pan.

"My disciplinary hearing at the Bar Association is scheduled for next Tuesday. I need to write a submission."

"Oh boy."

I raise my eyebrows. "Yeah. I could be looking for a new career by the end of next week. Do you think I'd make a good detective?" I try for cheerful but he isn't buying it.

"Would you like me to come with you?"

I'm about to say no but pause. "Why don't you let me think about it?"

He nods.

"You worried about it?" he says.

"The salmon?"

"The Bar hearing. Losing your license."

I toss the salad in a bowl and add some baby beets, get out a couple of serving forks.

"I don't want to stop being a lawyer if that's what you mean, but I misled the court and that's pretty bad."

"I've heard of lawyers who've embezzled clients' funds who got off with some nominal fine."

Frowning, I press the salmon with a fork, wondering if I've cooked it long enough. "Those types of mercenary sharks have friends in high places. That's not me."

"Who's going to represent you?"

I place the salmon on two dinner plates and take a seat next to him.

"Myself."

"You sure that's a good idea?"

"I want to. I think it will be good for the Committee to see that I'm genuinely remorseful." I smile at him. "Now, that's enough about me and the state of my sorry life, let's eat."

He gets the message, takes a mouthful of salmon, and looks thoughtful. "Want to meet my pop this weekend?"

"Your father?"

He nods. "I've got to go to the care home to do some gardening. Pop's got a balcony connected to his room and likes to sit out there when the sun is shining."

I'm touched he wants me to meet his father. "I'd like that very much, Ethan. Thank you for asking."

He smiles, goes back to the salmon.

"Good," he says between mouthfuls, grunting. "Really good."

I wonder whether he will stay overnight or play the gentleman. I think of telling him about my session with

Lorna and how I didn't perform the checking process as much today.

"I think from now on everything's going to be all right," I say, suddenly. "Me, I mean. I feel different."

He puts down his fork and kisses me. "I think so, too."

"Salmon breath," I say, laughing.

"Best kind of breath going."

*

He stays overnight. I lie in his arms listening to his gentle breath, feeling the warmth of his skin. I wonder how this is even possible. With so many bad things occupying my mind for so long, it's the strangest feeling to have such loving and happy thoughts, to believe in something steady and certain and trustworthy. Tonight, I feel like the luckiest girl alive.

His phone rings in the middle of the night. He murmurs into the phone, hangs up, then gets out of bed.

"What is it?"

"Sorry to wake you," he says, buttoning his shirt. "They found a body."

"Oh."

"Yeah. Welcome to my life."

I think yes, this is what it would be like, life as a cop's wife, to be roused in the middle of the night only for them to disappear for days on end while they get sucked into a vortex of an investigation.

"Homicide?"

He laughs. "Already planning the prosecution?" He sits on the end of the bed and puts on his shoes. "Short on details at the moment. Body found in Central Park, in the ravine, the stream valley section of the North Woods." He bends down and gives me a kiss. "Now you know about as much as I do, Counselor." He pauses at the door. "I'll call you later if I get a chance."

"Take care," I say.

After he's gone, I roll over and go back to sleep.

33

When I wake up, there's a text message from Ethan. *Wanted you to hear it from me first. Alistair Kennedy is dead.* I touch my throat, shocked. Alistair Kennedy? Ethan's text includes a news link so I click on that and read the article:

> *Teacher's body found mutilated. The body of Alistair Kennedy, 53, former Head of English at Ashbury Preparatory and Grammar School, was discovered in Central Park overnight. Police confirm witness accounts that the body was naked and the penis had been dismembered. No cause of death has been released so far. Kennedy had recently faced criminal charges of sexual assault against minors in his care but the case was dismissed due to a mistrial. Parents of the children involved in the allegations are currently being contacted and questioned by police.*

Rattled, I put down my phone. Although Kennedy was no great loss to society, his murder is still unnerving. Who could be responsible? One of the victims' parents? Claire? She was certainly angry enough about what had happened. But murder? What about Claire's husband, Susie's father, a man I had never met? According to Claire, he wasn't exactly afraid to resort to violence.

I consider phoning Claire. But what would I say? And the police would no doubt soon be in the process of questioning her, if they weren't already doing so, and contacting her might be seen to be interfering in a homicide investigation. I decide to wait until I've had a chance to speak to Ethan. Get more information.

Sometimes arrests are made early and all this could soon be resolved.

I need to get up and finish my hearing submission, so that's what I do, pushing all thoughts of Kennedy's death aside as best I can. I manage to focus for a good two hours, drafting and tweaking, until the chirp of my cell takes me out of the flow. I assume it's Ethan, but then I see my mother's number. I answer.

"Hey, Mom."

"Hello, hon…" She fades out. I hear a thumping motorbike. The blast of a car horn. Heavy traffic.

"Where are you, Mom? I can barely hear you."

"That better?" she says, raising her voice.

"Yes."

"Sorry, I'd forgotten how noisy the city can be."

"You're here? Why didn't you tell me you were coming?"

"I wanted to surprise you. Can you take some time out of your busy workday to have lunch with your mom?"

I swallow down guilt. I still haven't told her about my suspension. Lunch would probably be a good opportunity to come clean.

"I'd love to, Mom."

"You would? Oh good. What about that little deli near Brooklyn Bridge Park?"

"Sure, I remember that place. Miro Deli. Great salads." I look at my watch. A quarter after eleven. "I can be there at noon. That okay for you?"

"Perfect, hon. See you soon."

We end the call and I stand looking at my phone. Something's off. Something in my mother's voice I haven't heard before and I don't like it one little bit. I pull on my jacket, pick up my purse, and grab my keys. I pause there and look over my shoulder at the living room blinds, the windows, all the things waiting to be checked. Not this time, I tell myself. It's safe here. No one is getting in. The monster is dead. I open the door and leave.

34

It has been a while since I've been to Brooklyn Bridge Park, a beautiful spot with glorious views across the East River. I remember when the park was being constructed. As an associate for Winters, Coles and Partners, I had worked on planning permission for the development. It had been an ambitious project involving revitalizing 1.3 miles of Brooklyn's post-industrial waterfront, encompassing Atlantic Avenue, the Brooklyn Heights Promenade, and Jay Street north of the Manhattan Bridge. The site included piers, covered basketball courts, large grassy areas, a spectacular paved promenade, a marina, a grand carousel with beautifully crafted wooden horses, even a strip of golden sand along the shoreline for volleyball players.

Today the park is relatively free of people as I cut across a finely clipped grassy area, narrowly avoiding a galloping Labrador running for a Frisbee. I head along the promenade feeling more positive than I have in ages. The air smells salty. Fresh. It's good. I'd forgotten. Even the chill of the breeze is pleasant. I look out at the East River and watch the hydrofoil boats skip across the water.

When I arrive at Miro Deli, Mom is waiting for me at a window seat with views across to Manhattan. She looks tired. It's been at least six months since I last saw her. I feel an ache in my ribcage. I have been too wrapped up in myself and not much of a daughter lately.

When she sees me, a big smile breaks out across her face. She stands and pulls me into an embrace, nearly knocking the cane out of my hand. I smell patchouli and paint thinner.

"Oh, hon. It's so good to see you," she murmurs, hugging me tight.

She lets go and holds me at arm's length.

"You're skin and bones! You promised me you would take care of yourself."

"You should talk, Mom. There's not much to you either at the moment."

She waves me off.

"Shall we order?" she says, taking a seat to look at the menu. "The barley grain risotto with mushroom sounds good. I'm going to go with that. What are you going to have, hon?" She sounds cheery, artificially so, and I'm wondering, with ever-increasing dread, what she has in store for me.

"Haloumi salad, I think," I say, snapping the menu shut.

A waitress with dreadlocks looped in a topknot places a water jug on our table and takes our order. After she leaves, I fill our glasses.

"So what brings you to the city?"

Mom averts her gaze, shifts the paper napkin in front of her.

"I had an appointment."

"An appointment?"

She nods. "A medical one."

I frown. "Is there anything I should know?"

She shifts the paper napkin back to its original spot. "Actually, there is something I wanted to talk to you about."

My mouth goes dry. "You're worrying me here, Mom."

"Oh, honey." Her eyes well with tears.

145

"Mom, what is it? Please tell me."

Big fat tears drip down her face. She dabs them with her napkin.

"I've got ovarian cancer."

I think I might throw up. "What did you say?"

"I didn't know how to tell you. I've been having treatment for six weeks. You should get a check-up, hon. It's the type of cancer that took Nana May. It may run in the family." She pauses. "There are tumors."

"Oh God, Mom. No."

"They say with treatment, I might stand a chance."

"A chance?"

"Thirty percent."

I'm stunned. "Why didn't you tell me?"

"I didn't want to worry you. Not after everything you've been through."

I start crying. "Oh, Mom."

"It's not over yet, hon. I'm fighting this with everything I have."

We stare at each other. Thirty percent. I want to punch a wall.

I reach for her hand. "Promise me you'll tell me everything from now on," I say. "I want to be there for you."

She squeezes back. "I will."

She laughs, wiping her eyes. "Look at us, would you? Crying like two little girls."

The waitress with the dreadlock topknot arrives with our meals. She sees what a mess we're in. "You folks all right here? Want me to come back?"

"We're fine," says Mom. "We're ready to eat now. Aren't we, hon?"

146

35

My return trip home occurs in a daze. Cancer. Thirty percent chance of survival. Jesus. I glance around the half-empty train. I wish I was them. The young couple with a travel-worn backpack absorbed in a Lonely Planet guide. The two old ladies in knee-high pantyhose and sneakers conversing loudly in Polish. The Chinese man circling things in a folded copy of the *Sing Tao Daily*.

I want to tell all of them what just happened. But I don't. Instead I stare and say nothing.

One of the Polish ladies reminds me of Nana May. The happiest woman that ever lived. An elfin woman with a seemingly endless supply of positive energy who brought joy to everyone who knew her.

Then Nana May got sick and we all watched that good and happy woman be bought to her knees. She fought hard, tried to smile her way through the pain, but it was too much, even for Nana May. Her final weeks were lived in a cloud of morphine. She became a stranger, and bit by bit, the cancer swallowed her up until she was nothing more than a withered rubber suit.

I did not want that for my mother.

I think back to our conversation. I was the last person Mom had told about the cancer, that was obvious now, and that fact hurt a lot. My brother and sister, Becca and Danny, had known all along and supported her. But not me. I was too wrapped up in myself, too lost in my own wretched and futile neurosis.

Well, all that was going to change. I would do everything I could to help her. The first thing would be to make sure she was getting the best possible treatment. John Liber's wife was an oncologist. I would go talk to her, find out all the available options.

I stand as my train pulls into my stop. Thirty percent isn't nothing. Thirty percent is a fighting chance. And I would do my utmost to put my mother on the right side of the ledger.

I disembark and make my way up the subway steps and carry on to the park across the road from my apartment. Without thinking, I pause by the hedge line and start counting the floors. One. Two. Three. Four. It takes a minute to register what I'm doing. I clench my fists, frustrated. I want so badly not to do this anymore, but the compulsion to look is just too strong. For now, I give in and return my gaze to the apartment. Something's not right. The blinds are closed all the way. Surely I opened them this morning?

I rack my brain. After Ethan's text, I got out of bed and went straight to work on my submission on my laptop at the kitchen table. I guess it was possible I didn't bother opening the blinds, especially since I was also distracted with the news about Kennedy.

I wait awhile longer at the hedge line, just watching. The cat tiptoes across the roof, then leaps to the floor below. There doesn't seem to be any movement inside my apartment. Nothing to suggest anyone is there. Anyway, who precisely do I think is inside? Haven't I accepted the fact that Rex Hawkins is dead? Am I now inventing other phantom monsters to take his place?

I decide I'm being ridiculous. I will not let this disorder rule my life. Using my annoyance to propel me, I cross the road and go inside.

When I open the door to my apartment, I see that everything is fine. Yes, the blinds are down but everything else looks in order. I cross the floor and pull up the blinds and light floods the apartment. I pause by the window and look over at the park where I have just been standing.

My heart aches a little. How many hundreds of times have I stood there shaking with uncertainty and fear? How long is it going to take me before I can get on top of this miserable thing? I need to remember what Lorna said. There's no way to outrun it. It's going to be a long process and I need to be patient with myself. Getting worked up and frustrated is not going to help.

I turn from the window and shift my focus back to my mother. Before I contact John Liber's wife, it would be sensible to do some preliminary research on the latest ovarian cancer treatments.

As I reach for my laptop on the kitchen table, something catches my eye. A lone mug on the kitchen countertop. Not one of my usual ones but the "Happy it's Friday" mug that normally sits at the back of the cupboard. It wasn't on the counter this morning. I know this for sure.

I begin sweating. Maybe Ethan came around when I was out? But Ethan doesn't have a key. I inch forward and pick up the mug. When I see what's inside, I scream.

36

Inside the mug is a dismembered penis. I stare transfixed by the fat slug of a thing, not quite believing what I'm seeing.

"Hello, Amelia."

The hairs on my neck stand up on end. I turn. Rex Hawkins is standing there. Smaller than I remember. Diminished somehow. Late forties has given way to early fifties. Dark hair grayer at the temples. Lines chiseled deep around those deceptively friendly blue eyes. He's dressed much the same as the day he abducted me. Jeans, plaid shirt, meticulously clean and ironed to hard creases. But his once sun-burnished skin is now pale and dull. This is a man who now lives in the shadows. I start to shake. All I can think of is, I was right. I was right all along.

He chin-nods toward the mug. "Do you like my gift, Amelia? I know how badly you wanted that son-of-a-bitch put away."

My legs tremble as the cold hard reality hits. My worst fear is here, standing right in front of me.

"I'm not sorry he's gone," I say, surprising myself.

A flash of uncertainty crosses Rex's face. I turn and get myself a glass of water from the kitchen faucet.

"They told me you were dead," I say with my back to him. "They said they had your DNA."

When I look at him again, he's smiling. "And yet here I am."

I nod, getting it. "You used your money. Paid people off."

I move past him, carrying my glass of water, taking a seat on the sofa. My Glock is in the top drawer of the side table to the left. But if I go for it now, there's a good chance he'll intercept me.

He stares at me, contemplating. "You're different."

I take a sip of water and try to keep my voice from shaking. "What do you want?"

He moves to the living room window, half-sitting on the sill.

"But you've struggled, haven't you? I've seen it with my own eyes. I know you've tried to rebuild your life, and that is really very admirable, but it has been hard, hasn't it?" He pauses, waiting for me to say something. When I don't, he continues, "But on the bright side, there's a new man in your life. Detective Ethan North. Such an earnest and decent law-abiding man. A man who likes you on all fours apparently."

I feel violently ill. He pauses, watching me carefully.

He smiles. "Oh, yes, a very different Amelia."

He sits next to me. I can't breathe. Everything comes back in a rush. The forest. The rape. I don't want to show him how scared I am but I know I must be leaching it from every pore.

"You're shaking like a leaf," he says, touching my thigh.

I start to cry. "Please don't do this. I was just getting my life back on track."

I lift my hand to bat away the tears but he catches my wrist.

"Leave them," he instructs. "It's pretty."

I look at him, tears blurring my vision.

"Please, Rex. If you leave now, I'll never tell a soul you were here."

He scratches his chin and pretends to think it over, "Let me consider that for a moment." He lets out a breath. "No, I don't think so. I like being here with you too much."

I glance at the side table where my Glock is. He sees me looking.

"I know," he says, sighing. "You want your gun." My heart sinks. "You'd use it, too, wouldn't you? Put a bullet right between my eyes if you had half the chance."

Rex pulls my Glock from the small of his back and places it on his knee. I stare at the gun and feel sick. That was my very best chance of getting out of here alive.

"Take off your sock," he says.

I'm startled by his request. "My sock?"

"I want to see your foot."

Suddenly I'm angry. "No."

He gives me a sympathetic look. "Oh, you're shy."

He pauses and I think he's going to let it drop, but he doesn't.

Lightly, he touches the gun. "Please take it off, Amelia."

I hesitate. Inside I'm fuming. But what choice do I have? Swallowing down my humiliation, I slip off my special compression sock and expose my ugly, mangled foot to him. He crouches and does a 360 to get the full Amelia Kellaway semi-foot experience. He stares, fascinated. He's so close I can feel his breath on my skin. I think about kicking him in the face.

"I'm sorry that happened," he says, sitting down. "I read about it in the papers. Just like I read everything about you when you came back, including what you said about me."

I put my sock back on. I shoot a look at the front door. I could make a run for it, but that would mean wrangling with all the locks and he would get to me before then.

I need to think of something else so I stall for time. "There are others, aren't there? Innocent women you've killed."

Rex's face darkens. "Oh, you mean your wall of infamy."

"Shelly White. Amanda Buckley. Olivia Wendell. You murdered them just like you were going to murder me."

"You don't know what you're talking about," he says, eyes narrowing.

Emboldened, I carry on. "And what about the missing women? Last count puts them at seventeen. But there are more, aren't there? You can't stop. I feel sorry for you. It must be terrible to be so full of hate."

"That's enough now, Amelia." Rex stands and puts the gun back in his waistband. "It's time to go." He points to the kitchen table. "Turn on your laptop. You're writing a note."

I don't move.

He sighs as if dealing with a small child. "I know where they all live, Amelia. Every single one of them. All the people near and dear to you. All of the people you love in the world. Mother, Ruth Kellaway (and, yes, the envelope was from me), up in Rochester, in that quaint white and blue two-bedroom weatherboard house on Roberta Drive, such a nice laid-back community there, Amelia, so good for arty types like your mother. Your sister, Becca Tait, wife to Andy Tait, mother to little Nancy and Johnny Tait. Thanks to Andy's job in university administration, they've chosen to raise their growing young family in the nice safe city of Syracuse. They've got a swell bungalow they're in

153

the process of restoring. You should visit sometime, I'm sure they'd love to see you. Then there's Danny, your brother, and his lovely wife, Laura, and their new baby girl, Alice. They've just bought their very first house in a super neighborhood in Albany. There's a big backyard for little Alice to play in and good schools for when she grows up. Then closer to home, how could we forget Mr. Ethan North and his dear old father. Beth and her lovely new wife. Shall I keep going?"

My mouth goes dry. "No."

He turns the laptop to face me. "I'm glad we managed to reach an agreement. Password please."

Reluctantly I log on and tap keys as he dictates.

"Let's keep this short and simple. Dear friends and family, Please do not be concerned, but I need some time on my own to think. I have been going through a difficult time and feel that some space will do me good. I will return when I'm ready. Thank you for understanding. With love, Amelia."

I consider including a hidden message, but it's impossible with him standing over my shoulder. He pivots the laptop toward himself and reads.

"Good."

I get up. "I need to bring my foot meds with me. They're in my purse." He doesn't stop me as I cross the floor to retrieve my purse from the kitchen counter. My cell rings, startling us both. I snatch it from the counter. It's Ethan. I quickly hit accept and his voice fills the line.

"Amelia, you've got to get out of there! Rex Hawkins is alive! He killed Kennedy! We got a DNA hit from the crime scene."

"Ethan, he's here!"

154

Rex takes two steps forward, grabs the phone from me, and smashes it against the wall. He turns to me, his face twisted in anger.

"What a stupid thing to do."

He grabs my hair. I scream out in pain and he clamps his hand over my mouth. I struggle against his grip, my heels slipping against the tiled kitchen floor.

"You think you can get away from me, Amelia?" he hisses in my ear.

Behind me, I feel the cutlery drawer pressing into my back. I reach around and pull out a carving knife. Rex jumps back.

"Get the hell away from me," I splutter.

Rex holds up his hands. "Don't do anything reckless, Amelia."

"You're the reckless one, Rex. You got sloppy. DNA at the Kennedy crime scene? I expected better from you."

"Give me the knife."

"I will not."

"Don't make me hurt you. I don't want to hurt you."

I raise my voice. "Who the hell do you think you are? How dare you come into my house. How dare you threaten my family. How dare you threaten me."

He wipes his face with his hands and shouts, "Give me the fucking knife!"

"Ethan will be here soon. With reinforcements. You're going to prison for a very long time."

He rushes for me and I plunge the knife right into his chest. He yells and stumbles backward, and the knife sticks out of his body like some crazy Halloween party trick. I stare in disbelief at what I have done. Move, I hear the voice tell me. Move as fast as you can. So I do, snatching the Glock from in his waistband, then running down the hallway. Behind me I hear the tink of metal on metal as Rex tosses the knife in the sink, then the sound of his footsteps thundering after me. I make it to my bedroom and slam the door shut, my slippery, bloody hands fumbling with the lock, only just turning it closed before Rex shoulder-charges the door. I back away and watch the door bounce on its hinges.

"Amelia! Open the fucking door!"

I hold out the gun. The door breaks apart and Rex leaps through it, arms outstretched, ready to get me. I fire and the bullet flies into the timber frame above his head. I fire again but he's on me, batting the gun out of my hand, and the shot goes into the ceiling.

He slams me into the wall. "You think you can get away from me!"

I feel his hands around my neck, squeezing, crushing my windpipe. I claw at his fingers, shredding his skin, but his grip only tightens. Everything turns fuzzy at the edges. I'm losing consciousness. Somewhere in the back of my head, I hear a voice. So this is it. This is how you will meet your end. I stare into his cold black eyes, hoping to reach some hidden part of his humanity. But he is somewhere else far from here. I'm fading, the gray darkness is closing in. I'm so sad that Rex Hawkins's face will be the last thing I ever see.

I wake up alone in my bedroom, lying on top of my bed. My hands fly to my aching neck and I start coughing. God. It hurts so much. I swallow and groan in pain. But at least I'm alive.

I sit up and I'm hit with an almighty dizzy spell. I wait for it to pass. Take five deep breaths. Outside there are sirens in the distance. I pray they are coming for me.

"I never wanted it to be like this, Amelia."

I jump, startled by the sound of Rex's voice. I peer over the side of the bed and there he is, clammy and drained of color, propped up against the wall, his shirt soaked with blood.

"I'm sorry. I truly am," he says.

The sirens grow louder.

"There's no way out, Rex. They're almost here."

He nods sadly. He looks at me, face softening. "I miss my horses, Amelia. My ranch. My old life. You would have liked it there I'm sure." He winces and touches his wound. "You got me good, didn't you? You always were a fighter." He knocks the tip of the Glock against the wooden floor. "Why don't you come down here and sit next to me?"

"What are you going to do?" I say, feeling the dread flood my veins.

"Shoot you then myself? How about that?"

I can't speak.

"What? You don't like that option, Amelia? What would you like me to do? Hand myself in like a good ol' boy?" He smiles at my discomfort. "Of course you would. But how much fun would that be?"

Wincing, he shifts from his position against the wall and tries to stand. For a moment, he sways there on his knees then manages to raise himself upward. He waves the gun at me.

"Lie down."

I don't move.

"Go on. On your front, face into the pillow."

157

"No."

"Do as I say."

I shake my head. "I want to look you in the eye."

He stares at me.

"I sure am going to miss you, Amelia."

Tears burn my eyes. I think of my mom. I think of Ethan and how we made love in this bed.

"Just do it," I say.

"Goodbye, Amelia."

Then he turns and walks out the door. It takes me a moment to process what's happening. At first I feel relief. I'm alive. He didn't shoot me. I didn't die in my bed. But then it hits me. If he gets away now he'll be able to torment me whenever he likes. He'll be able to come and go whenever he pleases. He'll be like a mutating virus and I'll be like its long-suffering victim. I cannot let that happen.

I get off the bed and enter the hallway. "Wait."

Rex stops and turns. "What is…"

Before he can finish the sentence, I launch myself at him, using the weight of my body to tip him off balance, just as Beth taught me. We both crash to the floor and his head collides with the corner of the baseboard and he lets out a moan. I try to snatch the gun away from him but he's holding on too tight. Gritting my teeth, I jam my elbow into his wound as hard as I can and he screams in pain and loosens his grip. The gun falls from his hand, disappearing somewhere beneath us. We struggle for control, our bodies twisting and turning as we wrestle each other. I feel something pressing into my shoulder blade. I flip over and my fingertips touch the cool polymer exterior of my Glock.

There's pounding on the front door. They are here. Ethan is here.

Then something happens. My lips go numb. The world turns black and white at the edges. Oh no, not now. Please, God, not a blackout now. I'm half aware of Rex, getting to his knees, standing. The gun, where is my gun? Is it in my hand?

"What did you say?" he says.

I imagine pulling the trigger. Then I'm gone.

37

I am all alone in a beautiful walled garden. Quiet. Sunlit. A pool of crystal-clear water glimmers at its center. I lay naked on warm rocks, watching a northern breeze ripple through the treetops, listening to the hum of bumblebees, the whir of a hummingbird drawing nectar.

I am totally without fear. I am a marvel and all around me is a marvel too. The smell and sights of a good world. Then I see it. Encroaching on this sacred space. A snake, gliding through the grass, hissing its forked tongue, black beady eyes upon me. So I pick up a rock and smash in its head.

"Hey you."

My beautiful walled garden vanishes.

"Don't cry."

I open my eyes. Ethan's kind face is above me. I reach up and touch his cheek.

"You're safe now," he says.

I smell blood. I turn my head and see swirls of crimson on the floor, discarded bloody swabs and tissues scattered everywhere.

"Where am I? What happened?" My lips feel like two fat blisters.

I try to think back, to put everything in order. Nothing fits. My head pounds. I moan and press my hands to my skull. I try to sit up. Ethan gently pushes me back down.

"Can't you give her something for the pain?" he says to someone over my head.

I smell Lysol and latex, feel a tug on my arm, a prick on my skin.

"Amelia, they're going to lift you onto the gurney now. Okay?" Wheels squeak beside my head. Someone says one, two, three and up I go. Ouch. My arm.

"You okay? Is your arm sore? I think her arm's broken."

I glimpse the bloody swirls on the floor again. Then I remember.

"Rex," I say, sitting upright.

A hand lowers me back down.

"Lie flat, miss. You've knocked your head."

Ethan comes to me and holds my hand.

"I'm sorry for not believing you," he says.

I raise my bloody hands and look at them.

"I shot him?"

Ethan nods. They begin wheeling me out of the apartment.

"I'll follow in my car," Ethan says to one of the medics.

I grab Ethan's arm. "Did he get away?"

Ethan looks at me. "They're taking you to Bellevue. I'll meet you there."

I clutch Ethan's arm tighter. "Tell me, Ethan. Did he get away?"

He shakes his head. "No."

"Is he dead?"

"Amelia, we can talk about this later. You need medical treatment."

"I need to know, Ethan. Did I kill him?"

He hesitates, as if searching for the right thing to say. He glances back at the bloody mess on the floor. "He went into cardiac arrest twice but they stabilized him. Last I heard the son-of-a-bitch is still with us."

I feel bitter disappointment. "He's still alive?"

Ethan nods. He bends and kisses me on the forehead. "Now please let them take care of you."

They take me away, the three medics carrying me and the gurney down the stairs because the elevator with the scissor gate is too small. They wheel me into the back of the ambulance. I quietly exhale. I close my eyes and think.

Epilogue

The weekend away to Nantucket is Ethan's idea. He surprises me after work on Friday with an overnight bag, exactly one year after the incident with Rex Hawkins. Although Ethan makes no mention of this, I know, of course. Details like that are important to me.

I have a pile of work to do for an upcoming trial, so my first instinct is to say I can't go. But as I look at Ethan standing there, silly grin on his face, cheeks flushed with excitement and just a smidgen of pride, I decide that some things are more important than work.

We arrive on the island in the middle of a vicious squall. Rain batters the windshield of our rental as we hunt the backroads for the Airbnb Ethan booked. We finally locate it at Siasconset Beach, on the eastern end of Nantucket Island. A pretty one-bedroom cottage, set back from the beach on its own grassed section with unobstructed views of the ocean. Ethan and I go from room to room, charmed by the cozy décor. The old stone fireplace filled with sawed logs waiting to be lit. The ancient rolled-armed sofa covered in a hand-crocheted afghan. The clawfoot bath and wrought iron double bed covered with a handstitched settler's quilt.

I turn to Ethan. "Thank you for doing this."

He glances around, pleased with himself. "I did good, didn't I?"

I give him a peck on the cheek.

"Most definitely," I say.

He gives me a squeeze. "Why don't you take a bath while I light the fire and fix us something to eat."

We wake in the morning to an even worse storm. We linger in bed, pulling open the curtains of the large picture window to watch terrifyingly large waves crash wildly against the shore. As I lie there in Ethan's arms, safe in our little paradise, I have never felt such gratitude. This good and kind man has been my rock this past year, my lover and friend. I don't know what I would have done without him.

"Oh no, she's thinking," says Ethan. "I can hear the wheels turning."

I give him a playful tap on the arm. "They're happy wheels."

"Good," he says.

"Oh, I forgot to tell you. Mom called. She went for a check-up and her oncologist said her recovery is progressing nicely. He said he thinks Mom might be out of the woods."

Ethan gives me a squeeze. "That's great news."

By early afternoon, the sky brightens, clearing enough for us to venture out. Hand-in-hand, we amble through the quiet tree-lined streets, stop for a long lunch at the village, then head up Sconset Bluff Path. When we reach the lookout, we stop to admire the spectacular views. The vast Atlantic Ocean on one side, grand stately mansions on the other.

I notice Ethan shaking. At first, I think it's from the cold, then he drops to one knee and pulls out the ring.

He looks up at me. "Amelia Kellaway, will you do me the honor of marrying me?"

Suddenly I feel breathless. "Oh, Ethan."

"Say yes."

I nod and laugh. "Of course I will. Yes with all my heart."

He whoops loudly and jumps to his feet.

"Thank you," he says, slipping the ring on my finger and pulling me into an embrace. "You've made me the happiest man alive."

And then, on this most special of days, as I weep tears of joy, I think of him. Rex Hawkins. A poisonous black cloud hanging over me. Still alive. In prison and awaiting trial. But still alive nonetheless. And I think to myself that 366 days ago I should have killed that bastard when I still had the chance.

*

We are not long home from Nantucket on Sunday night when my cell rings. It's John Liber. Unusual for him to call at this hour.

"John?"

"There's been a development, kiddo."

My scalp pricks. "Sounds serious."

"Yeah." He lets out a breath. "There won't be a trial. Hawkins is going to plead guilty."

I laugh.

"For real," says John.

"I don't believe it."

"You're telling me. That's not all. He wants to talk about the other murders." My heart beats fast. "And the missing women."

"You're joking."

"Nope."

He pauses.

"John, what is it?" I say.

"There's a catch."

"I bet there is."

John clears his throat. "He'll only talk to you."

"Me?"

"Yeah." A few beats of radio silence. "You don't have to do anything you don't want to do, Am. No one would hold it against you, not after everything you've been through with this asshole."

I stand there, breathing.

"You want to think on it?" says John.

I look over at Ethan, my new husband-to-be, totally absorbed in peeling potatoes for our roast chicken dinner. He gives me a wink, then returns to his task. He'll want to get the potatoes just right, make sure there's not a trace of skin left anywhere, *so they get a nice crunchy crust like Pop used to make them.* My Ethan, such a particular, careful man. I look at the shiny new ring on my finger and think of the other women who aren't here to enjoy life with their beloved partners and children. All because of Rex Hawkins.

"Count me in."

THE END

More books you'll love from Deborah Rogers…

The Amelia Kellaway Series
Left for Dead
Coming for You
Speak for Me

Standalone Novels
The Devil's Wire
Into Thin Air

About the Author

Deborah Rogers is a psychological thriller and suspense author. Her gripping debut psychological thriller, The Devil's Wire, received rave reviews as a 'dark and twisted page turner'. In addition to standalone novels like The Devil's Wire and Into Thin Air, Deborah writes the popular Amelia Kellaway series, a gritty suspense series based on New York Prosecutor, Amelia Kellaway.

Deborah has a Graduate Diploma in scriptwriting and graduated cum laude from the Hagley Writers' Institute. When she's not writing psychological thrillers and suspense books, she likes to take her chocolate lab, Rocky, for walks on the beach and make decadent desserts.

www.deborahrogersauthor.com

Made in the USA
Coppell, TX
27 January 2022